"It's a little early now to talk about gold medals, Alex," Mrs. Lescu said.

"You're probably right," said Alex, "but I've always believed in aiming as high as I could."

"All very good—nice," Mrs. Lescu said, "but I want you should be more polished, more smooth."

"Like Dee, you mean," Alex said.

"Dee? Yes, she is very smooth and polished already. Other things she needs to work on."

Like not stealing my ideas for new routines, Alex thought.

As Alex left the office, she felt as if she were reaching the boiling point inside. She would show them. She would be a champion. She wasn't going to let Dee Winters or Cristina Lescu stand in her way . . .

Other Avon Books in the
GOING FOR IT series

MAKING WAVES
by A. C. Chandler

Coming Soon

SUMMER DREAMS
by Bill Gutman

OUT OF CONTROL
by Sam Bittman

BAREBACK
by Merrilee Steiner

THIN ICE
by E. M. Rees

Avon Books are available at special quantity discounts for bulk purchases for sales promotions, premiums, fund raising or educational use. Special books, or book excerpts, can also be created to fit specific needs.

For details write or telephone the office of the Director of Special Markets, Avon Books, Dept. FP, 1790 Broadway, New York, New York 10019, 212-399-1357. *IN CANADA:* Director of Special Sales, Avon Books of Canada, Suite 210, 2061 McCowan Rd., Scarborough, Ontario M1S 3Y6, 416-293-9404.

GOING FOR IT #2

Balancing Act
REBECCA LARSEN

AN AVON FLARE BOOK

GOING FOR IT #2—BALANCING ACT is an original publication of Avon Books. This work has never before appeared in book form.

AVON BOOKS
A division of
The Hearst Corporation
1790 Broadway
New York, New York 10019

Copyright © 1985 by Cloverdale Press/Jeffrey Weiss Group
Published by arrangement with Cloverdale Press/Jeffrey Weiss Group
Library of Congress Catalog Card Number: 85-90657
ISBN: 0-380-89900-0

All rights reserved, which includes the right to reproduce this book or portions thereof in any form whatsoever except as provided by the U.S. Copyright Law. For information address Cloverdale Press, 133 Fifth Avenue, New York, New York 10003.

First Flare Printing, November 1985

AVON TRADEMARK REG. U. S. PAT. OFF. AND IN OTHER COUNTRIES, MARCA REGISTRADA, HECHO EN U.S.A.

Printed in the U.S.A.

WFH 10 9 8 7 6 5 4 3 2

Balancing Act

Chapter One

"Look at this!"

Melissa's whisper to Alexandra Hays, better known as Alex, was a loud hiss that made Mrs. Westbrook look up from her desk at the front of the classroom.

Melissa had open a copy of *Gymnastics International* and was almost drooling over a spread of full-color photographs of Vera Filipova, the Soviet gymnast, doing a series of four back handsprings in a row on a balance beam.

Melissa, sitting at the desk across the aisle from Alex, reached across the space between them and slipped the magazine onto Alex's desk. Filipova did look magnificent, and just gazing at the photos made Alex breathe a little faster. When she looked at the Russian champion, she could almost feel that same dazzling, whirring buzzing that came into her head when she was turning and twisting through the air herself, and the final high she felt when she hit the beam perfectly in complete balance.

"I can do that," Alex muttered.

The girl sitting in front of Alex turned around. As she did so her silken mane of blond hair swung perfectly into place. It was Deirdre "Dee" Winters. Alex and Dee were the two top gymnasts at Olympic High. Alex, with her mop of curly, dark hair, was the daredevil of the two. She was always experimenting with new routines, although she was not always willing to take the time to smooth out the rough edges. Dee, who was not as audacious, had a neater, more polished style. Her performances were always characterized by beauty and grace.

First Dee looked at the magazine, then at Alex. "You've got a long way to go, Alex, before you're in Filipova's league," Dee said.

"So do you," Alex snapped back. She glared at her friend and roommate of the past two years. There was something about Dee that got on her nerves sometimes. But then, it was only natural, Alex thought, for two people so close in ability and both so competitive to rub each other the wrong way once in a while.

By now Mrs. Westbrook was standing and drumming her fingers on the top of her desk. "Girls—Alex, Dee, Melissa—could you save it for later?" she said. "Class is almost over. If you could just let the rest of the class have a little peace and quiet so they can start on their poems ..."

Alex looked again at the magazine and noticed that there were also pages of diagrams outlining exactly what it was that Filipova was doing. "I want to borrow this," she whispered to Melissa, who nodded her head.

Then she closed the magazine, slipped it in with her other books and papers, and tried to get back to writing haiku poems about blazing suns and winter winds.

"Before you leave," Mrs. Westbrook said, "I have an announcement to make: There will be a special assembly in the girls' gymnasium right after class. It's compulsory, and homeroom teachers will be taking attendance.

"If I were on the girls' gymnastics team," she added pointedly while staring at Melissa, Alex, and Dee in the back of the room, "I wouldn't want to miss this one."

Now what was that supposed to mean? Alex wondered. The "girls' gymnastics team"?

Two minutes later the bell rang. Melissa got to her feet and came around to Alex's desk. "You guys going over to the auditorium now, Alex?"

Alex nodded.

"I'll walk over with you," Melissa said. "Wait for me for a minute. I've got to ask Westbrook something."

"Honestly, Alex," Dee said as she watched the lithe girl in jeans and a pink sweatshirt with white, woolly sheep imprinted all over it go up to the front of the classroom. "Ever since Melissa got to Olympic High she's been following you around like a puppy dog. Aren't you getting sick of her?"

"She's okay," Alex said.

"That's because you think of her as a one-man Alexandra Hays fan club plus cheering section. Couldn't we ditch her just for once?"

Alex giggled. "Well, you know, it's hard when you're new at a school everyone else has been at for ages."

"C'mon," Dee said. "Let's get out of here." She pulled on Alex's arm.

She tugged a second time, and Alex let herself be dragged out of the classroom. When they were out in the hall, Alex stopped. "I feel mean doing this," she said.

"Oh, come on," Dee said, tossing her hair back

and twisting her almost baby-doll-perfect features into what Alex would call a pout.

But she looked fabulous, anyhow, Alex thought, the way she always did—with a complexion that never broke out in pimples, thick hair that looked like something out of a fashion magazine, and rosy coloring that was set off perfectly by the pale peach-colored sweater she was wearing.

They saw the door of Mrs. Westbrook's classroom start to open, and Dee froze. "Good grief, Alex, now we'll never get away."

Then Dee moved in a flash and grabbed the handle of the door of a storage closet that was right in front of them. She pulled it open, tugged Alex's arm, and pushed her inside with her.

There they were, alone in total darkness with what seemed to be several sets of mops and pails.

"Dee, what are you trying to do?" Alex asked.

Dee was doing her best to muffle her giggles with a hand over her mouth.

"Shhh," she hissed at Alex. "I hear her coming."

Out in the hall Melissa was calling for them: "Alex, did you leave? Dee?"

Her calls grew fainter and fainter. She had obviously given up and was heading out to the auditorium.

"Dee, that was cruel!" Alex said.

"I know," Dee said. "It's just this crowded feeling she gives me. She never leaves you alone. Let's just wait in here for a couple of minutes, then we can take off. We'll probably meet her down at the auditorium, anyway, and she'll be all over you again as usual."

"It's creepy in here," Alex said. "I can't see a thing."

She groped in the blackness for the door handle and pushed. Nothing gave. "Is this the door?" she asked Dee.

"What do you mean, 'Is this the door'?"

"I just mean, if this is the door, it's stuck or something."

"It can't be stuck."

"Try it yourself."

Dee fumbled around and found the knob that Alex had been holding. She turned and pushed. "It won't budge," she said. "I can't stand this another minute. I hate the dark! I hate closets!"

Her voice was turning into a squeak.

"Calm down," Alex said.

She ran her hands down the wall and found a light switch. "There," she said as the lights went on, "now you're not in the dark anymore. You're just locked in a closet."

"I'll bet Melissa did it," Dee said. "She knew we were in here and she locked us in somehow."

"You're just suffering guilt pangs. She didn't come anywhere near this door, and besides, she wouldn't have done it, anyway."

"Well, what are we going to do?"

"I sort of thought," Alex said, "that since you got us in here, you might have some ideas about how to get us out."

"I don't hear anybody out there, do you?" Dee asked. She rested her ear against the door. "I think they're all down in assembly. Maybe if we yelled . . ." Dee cupped her hands and put them against the door. "Help!" she yelled. "Help—we're trapped in here!"

There was no answer.

"Nobody's out there," Alex said. "Maybe if we shouted out the window . . ."

She walked over to the window on the opposite

wall from the door. A couple of pushes and she had it open.

The lawn below the combined administration-classroom building was as empty as if it were Christmas vacation. "I don't see anybody down there, either. I guess they're all in the auditorium by now."

"This can't be happening to me!" Dee shrieked. "I hate closets, I hate elevators! I freak out when I'm trapped in small places!"

Alex was still leaning out the window. "Hey," she said, "there's a balcony right under this window on the next floor. I think it's right outside Mr. Amundsen's office. It's only about a story below. I bet I can drop down from here pretty easily and get onto it. Even if the window's shut, there's bound to be some secretary or someone sitting around down there who'll let me in."

Dee rushed to the window and looked out. "You can't do that," she said. "You might fall and kill yourself. That's crazy."

"Listen," Alex said, "I do crazier things than that every day, six hours a day—in a gymnasium. This will be a snap."

She had already forced the window all the way open and was putting one foot up on the sill. Dee pulled her back.

"Don't do it, Alex."

"You want to try?"

"No way."

"You want to spend the next six hours and maybe the whole night in this closet? You know that after assembly everybody'll go to the gyms for practice. Nobody'll show up here until some janitor comes up in the wee hours to sweep the floors."

"Well, since you put it that way . . ."

"Okay," Alex said. "I'll go down there and get in the window. Then I'll hunt up the janitor so he can come back up here and open the door."

"Be careful . . ."

Alex climbed onto the windowsill, grabbed it with both hands, and swung out. Hanging straight from the sill, she reached down slightly and caught hold of a pipe about a foot or so below.

Now that she was actually hanging there, it didn't seem as easy as it had when she had just been looking out the window. Maybe she had taken on more than she could handle. "You've got a habit of doing that, don't you, Alexandra?" she muttered to herself.

"What did you say?" Dee hollered down.

"Nothing," Alex said, breathing a little heavier. It'll be okay, she told herself. She just had to be very careful, very accurate.

It was a little like performing on the uneven bars, except she knew for sure that the uneven bars would hold her, and she wasn't so sure about this pipe.

With her tennis shoes she felt for cracks in the bricks that she could use to toe her way down the wall a little bit.

"Here goes!" she yelled back up to Dee, who was leaning out the window. Alex let go and dropped smoothly and easily on the balls of her feet onto the balcony, just outside the office of the headmaster of Olympic High—ex-runner Ralph Amundsen.

"It *was* a snap," she said, and waved at Dee, now some fifteen feet above her.

Through the window she could see a black-haired woman standing in the lobby outside Mr.

Amundsen's office. She tapped on the glass. The woman stared at her but didn't move.

"Hey, in there," Alex yelled as loudly as she could while knocking again. "Can you let me in? I'm trapped out here."

Now the woman walked toward her, and Alex could see that there was also a teenage boy sitting in a chair nearby.

"Excuse me," Alex said as the woman walked closer, "but could you please let me in?"

It was a large sliding glass window, and the woman unlatched it and pushed it open.

"What in world is this?" she asked as Alex stepped into the room. "Dropping down from the sky like bird?"

"I can't stop to talk now," Alex said. "There's someone trapped upstairs, and I've got to get her out. I have to find the janitor. Do you know where he is?"

"I do not know what you are talking about. How you got out there?"

Alex noticed that the woman had a foreign accent, not thick enough to make it hard to understand her English but still obvious.

Her clothes looked different to Alex too. There was nothing wrong with them, exactly—they were just a little plain-looking and cut sort of differently. The woman wore a simple, heavily starched white blouse with boxy short sleeves, like something someone would wear with a military uniform, and a dark gray skirt. She was short and slightly plump—but solid-looking, not flabby. She wasn't one of the teachers, Alex knew. Maybe she was one of the kids' mothers. Or could she have something to do with the janitorial staff?

But then, she didn't seem to know where the janitor was. . . .

"How you got on that balcony?" the woman asked again.

"I was stuck in a closet upstairs," Alex said. "We couldn't get the door open. So I opened the window and jumped down."

The woman ducked out on the balcony to look up at the window. Dee wasn't looking out the window anymore, Alex noticed when she looked. She'd probably gone back to the door to wait for her rescuers.

"That is ridiculous," the woman said. "You might have injured yourself. Stupid thing to do."

"You don't understand," Alex said. "I'm a gymnast. This was nothing for me. I do this all the time."

"Oh, really," said the woman, pulling her lips together into a rigid line.

"You know, gymnastics—that sport where you swing on bars and walk on a balance beam and stuff."

"Is that so?" the woman said. "You mean on thin little board, like circus tightrope?"

"Right, only I can't talk about it anymore right now," Alex said, thinking that the woman was not the parent of a gymnast, for sure, or she'd be more knowledgeable about the sport. "I've got a friend upstairs who's stuck in the closet. I have to get her out. You don't know where the janitor is, do you?"

Alex looked in the direction of the teenage boy this time. He shook his head. His clothes looked sort of odd, too, but he had an even smile; thick, curly hair; and big dark eyes. Although he was sitting, she could tell that he was fairly tall.

"I'll have to go look for him, I guess," Alex said, and dashed out the door.

It took her five minutes to track down the janitor and another five for him to take a screwdriver to the doorknob and release Dee from the closet. Thank goodness he didn't ask many questions.

Dee burst out of the closet. She was panting heavily, and strands of cobwebs clung to her hair and clothes.

"Oh, thank you, Alex. You did it. You were wonderful."

"Just make me one promise," Alex asked. "Don't try to get away from Melissa anymore."

"I solemnly promise to be kinder to Melissa," Dee said, holding up her hand with two of her fingers crossed. "Now we've got to burn to the auditorium."

The two of them ran down the stairs. "I hope we can catch at least a few minutes of this thing, whatever it is," Dee said.

"And I hope we don't get in trouble for our closet caper," Alex added. "Some strange woman was in Mr. Amundsen's office, and she wasn't too thrilled about my crash landing on the balcony."

Chapter Two

Alex had expected the assembly to be well under way by the time they arrived at the auditorium. But when they got there, nothing was happening except that a lot of kids were cruising the aisles, talking to their friends, while teachers tried to get them to sit down.

Miss Anderson, their homeroom teacher, bustled over as soon as she saw them come through the door. "Where have you girls been?" she snapped. "We've all been waiting, and Mr. Amundsen sent some boys out to look for you."

"For us?" Alex asked. "Why?"

"The whole girls' gymnastics team has to be here for this," Miss Anderson said. "Go right up to the front. Your group is sitting in the first row."

Alex and Dee took their seats while Miss Anderson walked over to Mr. Amundsen, who was standing talking to a group of teachers. After a few words with Miss Anderson, Mr. Amundsen walked up the steps to the auditorium stage and went behind the curtain.

Melissa was sitting two or three seats away from them. "Where have you guys been?" she asked. "I've been looking all over for you, Alex. Miss Anderson was throwing a spaz about this."

"What's the big deal?" Alex said. "They never held up things on my account before."

"I think it has something to do with Coach Baer," Melissa said.

Mr. Amundsen came out from behind the curtain and went up to a microphone at a podium on the side of the stage.

Alex looked back over her shoulder at the rest of the auditorium. Almost every seat was filled. The whole student body was there, apparently—all the kids on all the teams that represented nearly every sport featured in the Olympics. They came from all over the U.S. to Olympic High, a private boarding school in Colorado, because they knew that here they would have the best chance to hone their sports skills and, if they were good enough, eventually hit the Olympics. There were lots of sports schools that promised to do the same thing for young athletes, but Alex knew, as did the rest of the kids, that only the very best got picked to go to Olympic High.

On a wall high above where the students were sitting hung one of the largest portraits Alex had ever seen. It was a painting of Hamilton Ives, the founder of the school.

At age twenty-one Ives had gone to the 1924 Olympics in Paris, where he won a gold medal in the ten-event decathlon. When he died in 1977, he left twenty million dollars to the U.S. Olympic Committee to start Olympic High. The committee members ended up picking a three-hundred-acre tract of land in Colorado, and there they built some of the most complete and elaborate sports facilities in the world. And they hired the best coaches money could buy—like Ralston "let's hold it down. As Coach Baer said, this is a time when our team needs the very best leadership, so when we found out that he was leaving, we knew we had to find someone of the highest caliber, because only a person at the very top of the sport could hope to fill his shoes.

"Gymnastics in America is changing. What was once the underdog of sports in this country is now charged with new dynamism. We're sure we've hired someone as coach of our girls' team who's going to carry on the fine tradition of Coach Baer and who's also going to add new life and perspective to our training.

"This is a woman who has made headlines around the world with the young women whom she has taken to the Olympics. This is a woman who has made great personal sacrifices to be with us today, a woman who has given up much in order to come here and make a contribution to American gymnastics...."

Out in the audience, in the front row, and, in fact, in the entire auditorium, there was complete silence.

Dee passed Alex a note scribbled in pencil: "Who do you think it is?"

Alex shook her head.

Miss Anderson, sitting two seats away, reached over and grabbed the piece of paper out of Alex's hand, crumpled it up, and stuck it in her purse.

". . . And so," Mr. Admundsen concluded, "it is my great pleasure to introduce to you Cristina Lescu, former coach of the Romanian women's gymnastics team."

There was scattered applause as a woman stepped out from behind the curtain to join Amundsen at the podium.

"Good grief!" Alex gasped. "It's that woman I told you about—the one who was in Amundsen's office, the cleaning-woman type."

"You'd better shut up," Dee muttered. "She's going to hear you. We're in the front row, you know."

The woman had added a severe-looking gray jacket to her outfit now, Alex noticed. To her Cristina Lescu looked more like the warden of a women's prison than a coach. Alex shivered. This wasn't going to be one bit like being coached by Ralston Baer. How would someone like Cristina Lescu hit it off with someone like Alexandra Hays—wild about gymnastics, ready to try anything, but a little bit disorganized?

"She looks so unhappy," she whispered to Dee. "It's as if she's forcing herself to smile."

And where was the teenage boy she had seen with the woman? Alex wondered.

"Mrs. Lescu has brought with her her son, Danut," Mr. Amundsen said. "He will be attending Olympic High as do the teenage children of other teachers on our staff. I know that all of you will make a real effort to give Danut a very warm welcome."

Mr. Amundsen extended his arm toward the third or fourth row of the audience, and the tall, dark-haired boy Alex had seen earlier stood up and nodded at the audience.

"Mrs. Lescu, would you like to say a few words to our students?" Mr. Amundsen said.

She leaned toward the microphone. "I very happy to be here today," she said. "This new post means much to me. I am anxious to getting to work and meeting all of you. Thank you."

By now the audience was buzzing and whispering again.

"Have you heard of her before?" Melissa asked Alex and Dee.

"I've heard of her," Alex said. "I may have even seen her before at some meet or other, but I can't remember. How do you think she ended up here?"

"I think I read in the paper that she left Romania, but I thought she was going to be coaching someplace else in Europe," Dee said.

"What in the world are we going to do without Teddy?" Alex groaned. "This is going to be terrible."

"How can you say that, Alex?" Dee said. "I think this is one of the greatest things that's ever happened to Olympic High. Having her here won't just get us into the Olympics. This could mean we'll come home with everything—covered in gold."

"But Teddy was so wonderful."

"Teddy was too soft. He was pretty good for the United States, but when you talk about international competition, he didn't cut the mustard."

Mr. Amundsen tapped on the microphone. "Could we have a little quiet in here?" he asked. "I know this is a wonderful surprise as well as being a big shock about Coach Baer's leaving. But we'll all have plenty of time to talk about it soon enough.

"After our meeting here today and before any practices begin for the afternoon, we're all going to head out to the Student Center for a reception in the main hall. There each of you will have a chance to talk to Coach Baer and wish him well and to welcome the Lescus to our school."

After the assembly everyone filed into the Student Center. As Melissa, Dee, and Alex grabbed some hors d'oeuvres off a tea table, Mike Schultz, whom Alex had been dating since the year before, walked up to greet them.

Mike was on the boys' gymnastics team, and when he was around, it was usually hard for Alex to think about anything else. But today her mind was on the coaching change.

"This is really something, isn't it?" Mike said. "Wow, I can't believe it. I never thought Coach Baer would leave."

"Neither did we," the girls chorused.

"I wonder how she's going to like all of us," Alex said. "What she'll think of us."

"She'll like *you* just fine, Alex. You're the star of the team. She must have seen some of those articles about you in the newspapers. Remember that reporter last month who called you a 'pixie dynamo' and 'as perky as champagne bubbles'?" Melissa said.

"Wow, Melissa," Dee said, "give us a break! Alex doesn't need a scrapbook for her clippings as long as she's got you around."

"Dee, cool it," Alex said. "I appreciate that, Melissa, but I'm a little worried about this. Maybe we could just hang back here at this end of the room, have some shrimp cocktail, and duck out without anybody noticing. Then, by the time we get around to meeting her, she might have forgotten all about my balcony routine this afternoon."

"What are you talking about?" Mike asked.

"Yeah, what happened to you after class, anyway?" Melissa asked.

"It's too long a story to tell you now," Alex said.

Suddenly Coach Baer came up behind Alex and put his hands on her shoulders. "Surprised?" he asked.

"*Stunned* is more like it. This is awful," Alex said. "What are we going to do now?"

"You're going to do just fine."

"What I want to know is," Alex said, "did they make you do this somehow? Are they forcing you to leave?"

"Let's just put it this way," Coach Baer said. "It was sort of a mutual decision. Mrs. Lescu was available. They knew it, I knew it, and I knew what they wanted—so I took certain steps before they did. Anyway, we've all got to retire sometime."

"Oh, no," Alex said. "They can't do that to you."

"We're really going to miss you," Mike said.

"You've been a great coach," Dee said.

"Thanks, kids. But now it's time for all of you to meet Mrs. Lescu."

"What's she like?" Melissa asked.

"I haven't spent that much time with her, but from what I've heard, she's really a top coach who pays a lot of attention to detail and form but is also willing to try new things. You know, she's been through a lot. She's a defector. She and her son walked into the British embassy and asked for asylum while she was attending a meet in Holland."

"I don't think we want to go up there," Alex said.

"I do," Dee said.

"C'mon," said Coach Baer, and he nudged Alex

forward through the press of kids toward the reception line at the front of the hall.

They got in line and inched their way forward until Coach Baer, Alex, and Dee were right in front of Mr. Amundsen and Mrs. Lescu.

Mrs. Lescu's face was perspiring, and between handshakes, she pressed a handkerchief with embroidered initials to her forehead.

"This is a very exciting day for me," she said to Coach Baer.

Coach Baer put one hand on Alex's shoulder and one on Dee's. "Mrs. Lescu," he said, "I want you to meet the two top gymnasts on the girls' team of Olympic High. Right here is Deirdre Winters, but we call her Dee, and this is Alexandra Hays. Everybody calls her Alex."

He patted Dee on the shoulder and Alexandra on top of her brown, permed curls.

Mrs. Lescu looked first at Dee and then at Alex. She wasn't smiling now, Alex noticed. She reached out her hand first to Dee. "So nice meeting you, Miss Winters," she said.

Then she reached out to shake Alex's hand. "And this young woman, Miss Hays, I have already met, I believe."

She looked straight into Alex's eyes, and Alex felt as if her knees were going to crumple under her.

"Miss Hays is the daring young woman on balcony, I believe. You found janitor, yes?"

"Yes," Alex said quietly.

"I am so happy for you."

Mrs. Lescu turned away from them and looked down the row to take the hand of the next person in line.

Her son, Danut, was still looking at Alex and

smiling, though. "That was strange," said Coach Baer. "What was all that business about the balcony?"

"I don't know," Alex lied. "I'm not exactly sure."

Chapter Three

It was three days later when Mrs. Lescu actually took over the girls' gymnastics team.

Before that, the team had thrown a small going-away party for Coach Baer, who insisted he wanted to be out of the way before the new coach stepped in.

Every day, as usual, had been a full one for Alex and the rest of the team: ballet lessons to increase flexibility and stretch the muscles; weight training to develop strength; three or four hours a day of regular classes; and about five hours of gymnastics training.

"Do you think she's going to hold that incident on the balcony against me?" she asked Dee one afternoon as they practiced on the uneven parallel bars.

"You're taking all this much too seriously, Alex," Dee said. "Just relax and do your best and you'll be fine."

"But you don't understand. Her personality and my personality just don't fit together very well. I can tell. I'm the kind of person who likes things run in a loose sort of way. That's what makes me do my best. If I'm working for someone who's rigid, who corrects me all the time, I get afraid to try anything new. I just need a lot of love and encouragement, like Teddy used to give us. Then I can really blossom."

"I don't see how you can tell so much about Cristina Lescu just from meeting her once the other day. You've hardly even talked to her."

"You know what those coaches from Eastern Europe are like—you've seen them at meets. They never smile, and when someone finishes a routine, if there's some mistake or something, they always look like they're ready to ship the offender off to Siberia."

"Well, that's just because they have so much riding on every performance. The kids *have* to do well or the coaches could lose their jobs. Maybe that's one reason why Mrs. Lescu wanted to come to this country. Maybe she was tired of all that garbage and wanted to loosen up or something."

"That doesn't seem too likely to me. And this was just about the time when I wanted to get started on developing a new routine for the balance beam."

"What's wrong with your old one?"

"Nothing. I just got some new ideas from that magazine that I borrowed from Melissa the other day—from those pictures and diagrams of Filipova. I figure that if I get started now, I could have it ready just in time for the Nationals. But how in the world am I going to get all that off the ground with some new coach around?"

"Well, balance beam is your best event. You shouldn't have any trouble convincing her you're ready for something new."

"Maybe."

"Hey, I'd like to have another look at that magazine too. Maybe I could pick up something I could use. Could I see it?"

"I've got it in my locker. I'll show it to you after practice."

On the Saturday morning when the gymnastics team was supposed to work out for the first time with Mrs. Lescu, Alex awoke with a jolt when the clock radio's music went on at seven A.M.

"I don't want to go," she muttered to Dee.

"Don't be ridiculous."

They got up, dressed, and left the girls' dorm for the cafeteria, which was about half a block across the campus. Winter had already begun to touch the lawns and trees, and Alex shivered at the sharp bite of the wind, which seemed to penetrate her wool jacket.

She could hardly eat her breakfast, and the English muffin and bit of scrambled egg she did manage to swallow seemed to lie in a lump at the bottom of her stomach.

Melissa met them in the cafeteria, and the three girls walked over to the gym together. First they went into the locker room to change.

"Rats," Alex said to Melissa as she pulled on her favorite leotard, which was pale blue with white trim around the throat and sleeves. "Look at this hole," she exclaimed, indicating a spot at the waistline in the back where the stretchy material had worn so thin that now there was a gaping hole. "I've only had this thing for a month, and it's already worn-out. I must have caught it on something."

"Don't you have anything else to put on?" Melissa asked.

Alex peered in her locker. "All the other leotards in here are just about as bad; my good ones are in the wash back at the dorm."

"Well, here," Melissa said. "I've got a safety pin you can use to pull it together. Do it from underneath, then nobody will notice."

Alex accepted the pin and pulled the material around the hole together. It didn't work too well, but it was better than nothing, she figured. Something told her it wouldn't be a good idea to show up at the first practice with the new coach with a hole in her leotard.

Just as they were about to go out into the gym, they heard a buzzing noise come out of a loudspeaker in the locker room. "What's that?" Dee asked.

"I think somebody's trying to use the public-address system."

After a few blips the voice of Cristina Lescu came booming out into the locker room. "Dressing time is over. Now is time to assemble in the gymnasium for practice."

Dee giggled, but Alex shook her head. "I knew it was going to be like this," she wailed.

The fifteen girls who made up the gymnastics team filed into the gym where Mrs. Lescu was waiting in a khaki-colored warm-up suit with a clipboard in hand and a whistle hanging from a cord around her neck.

"Good morning, young women," she said, and motioned them to sit in the bleachers at the side of the gym.

Usually there was a lot of talking and laughing as everyone assembled in the gym. This time, however, there was total silence, Alex noticed.

"I have few words to say to you this morning about how I conduct business," Mrs. Lescu said.

"You are all very talented young women, and I know that you work hard for a long time now. But in next few weeks you will work more seriously than ever you have in your life. You will pay attention to details that you never notice before. You will be pushing yourselves to limits of your endurance.

"Now, to start, please everyone line up in straight line—right here," she said, indicating a painted line on the gym's wooden floor.

The girls stood up and filed into position as the coach looked up and down the line.

"From now on," she said, "practices run one half hour longer than usual for Saturdays."

No one said anything, but Alex could hear sighs up and down the line.

"From now on," Mrs. Lescu said, "we will also have inspection of your appearance every Saturday. And on Saturdays everyone is wearing team suit to practice. Other days, okay to wear what you want. But on Saturdays we look our best."

With that, Mrs. Lescu started to walk down the front of the line. She looked each girl up and down, from head to toe. Stopping in front of Angela Avery, she tugged at the corner of the pair of pink gymnast's trunks that Angela was wearing under her leotard. "This is fatal mistake," she said.

In front of another girl whose hair looked uncombed, she stopped again. "Let us have our hair done, just the way that we want it to look in competition, please," Mrs. Lescu said.

Alex felt as though the safety pin were burning a hole in her back.

Then Mrs. Lescu started walking down the line, looking at them from the back.

She hesitated slightly when she got behind Alex but then moved on. Alex breathed a sigh of relief.

"All right, everyone," Mrs. Lescu said. "First we do warm-ups, then we have some of you demonstrate for me what you can do."

After about an hour of warm-ups they took a break, and the coach went off to the team office.

"This is horrible," Alex told Dee. "I can't stand her!"

"She is pretty tough," Dee said. "She really came down hard on Angela about her outfit."

"I can't believe this," Melissa said. "The difference between her and Coach Baer is so incredible."

"Ooooh, I want him back so badly," Alex moaned.

"Well, it ain't gonna happen," Dee said. "Mrs. Lescu is here to stay, and we might as well make the best of it."

After the break the coach started going around to various areas of the gym to watch the girls go through their individual workouts, and Alex could see that she was taking notes about everyone on her clipboard.

She got to Alex just as she was practicing on the balance beam. "So, Miss Hays," she said. "Now we see if you are as good in gym as you are making flying leaps from windows."

Mrs. Lescu smiled, and Alex wondered if that was supposed to be a joke. All she knew was that she was getting off to a terrible start with this woman, but she didn't know exactly what to do about it.

For the first minute or so things went perfectly. Alex took a couple of deep breaths, mounted the balance beam gracefully, then moved quickly through some tumbling passes intermixed with dance movements. Her stomach muscles felt nice and tight. Her hips were perfectly in line with the beam.

Her handstands, her turns, her splits, her cartwheels, her flips were just right. She was really beginning to get into her routine. She felt all right. She posed elegantly with one arm extended overhead and then started a simple walk down the beam. That's when she felt a tiny prickling in her back. The safety pin had come open! She lost her concentration, and as she went into a leap she could feel herself losing her balance too. She bobbed a bit and slipped as she came out of the leap. But she caught herself before she went down completely and was able to pull back to a standing position. Beads of perspiration broke out on her forehead. She couldn't even look in Mrs. Lescu's direction.

It was time for the dismount, and as she came off the beam in a final double-back, she felt something going wrong as she twisted through the air. She stumbled as she hit the mat and threw up her arms awkwardly.

"Thank you, Miss Hays," Mrs. Lescu said, and Alex could see that she was furiously taking notes.

"I really messed up," Alex told Melissa a few minutes later. "That dumb safety pin came undone right in the middle of my routine!"

"Maybe you should tell her that," Melissa suggested. "It's bad enough performing in front of her for the first time without a pin jabbing you in the back. I didn't do so hot, myself."

Alex sighed. "It wasn't just the pin. She makes me nervous. We've performed in front of thousands of people lots of times, and I never felt like this. What is it about her that makes me screw up?"

Alex looked across the gymnasium and could see Mrs. Lescu watching as Dee performed on the uneven parallel bars. It looked as though Dee were doing a flawless job with her usual smooth, clean grace. A little too careful and cautious, perhaps, Alex thought, but definitely a solid performance. Dee did a somersault down off the uneven bars and landed on her feet in a beautiful position. Mrs. Lescu clapped her hands in a little bit of mock applause and then patted Dee on the back.

"Excellent form, Miss Winters," she said.

"Well, Dee seems to be getting off to a smashing start, doesn't she?" Alex said to Melissa.

"I'll say."

Dee came running up to them. "I think I did that the best I've ever done it. Did you see me?"

"It was terrific." Alex tried to pump as much enthusiasm into her voice as she could. "You did a super job."

"The coach seemed to like it, didn't she?"

"She even clapped for you," Melissa said.

"I guess she's not so bad, after all," Dee said. "She seems to appreciate good work."

Dee wandered off and stood next to Mrs. Lescu as she watched Beth Schmidt doing her floor exercises.

Pretty soon Alex could see that Dee was chatting with the coach about something. Then they both started laughing together.

"Do you believe that?" Alex muttered.

At lunchtime everyone went into the locker room to shower before heading for the cafeteria.

Alex stopped off at Mrs. Lescu's office on the

way. She stood in the doorway for a minute before the coach looked up and saw her there.

"Mrs. Lescu," she began.

"Yes."

"I don't know how to put this, exactly, but I feel as if I haven't gotten off to a very good start with you. Partly because of all that business at the headmaster's office the other day."

Mrs. Lescu said nothing. She just gave Alex the same intense gaze she had fixed on her that day in the reception line.

"I am a hard worker," Alex said. "And I do want to do my best for you. I'm very anxious to put a lot into my routines in the next few months to prepare for the Nationals in the spring. I expect to do very well."

"I expect everyone here to do very well."

"I'm sure we all will. Anyway, I just wanted you to know that."

"Thank you, Miss Hays. I appreciate that you come to talk to me."

As she left the office Alex wasn't so sure about that.

Chapter Four

Danut Lescu showed up in Alex's classes the Monday after the first practice with Mrs. Lescu.

It turned out that he was in all four of the classes that she had to squeeze into every morning: English, math, chemistry, and French.

She had gone early to math, the first class of the day, in hopes of finishing up some questions on a trigonometry assignment before the teacher got there. And there was Danut, the only other person in the classroom. He was thumbing through some of his new books.

For a moment Alex was tempted to duck back out the door and leave. She wasn't sure she could handle another dose of the Lescu family so early in the morning.

But he had already looked up and seen her, and she was afraid that if she left, she might offend him as well as his mother.

That morning he was wearing a stiffly starched white shirt with a striped tie, baggy charcoal-gray woolen slacks, and black leather shoes.

Alex looked down at her own violet-colored sweatshirt, blue jeans, and scuffed tennis shoes and shook her head.

She charged bravely up to a seat next to Danut, sat down, and opened her book.

"Good morning," he said.

"Good morning."

"You are Alexandra Hays," he said, smiling. "The girl from the balcony."

"Right."

He laughed.

Actually he wouldn't be bad-looking, Alex thought, if he didn't dress so oddly and if he got a decent haircut. As it was, his dark curls sort of stuck out in all the wrong places.

"You all set to start school?"

"I suppose so," he said. "I have been most anxious to come to the United States, and I was a little worried that I would not know everything high school juniors know in your country. But now that I look through these books, I think I will do all right."

"You're a junior too?"

"I think so, but I am hoping next year I go to college—Harvard or Yale. Mr. Amundsen helps me with the applications and the tests. He believes my background helps me get into the premedical program at one of those great schools. Mr. Amundsen also arranges that I take extra science classes at your community college while other students are doing training."

"I should get you to help me out with my chemistry sometime. You must be a very good student."

"I am not sure," he said. "Is very different to compete against students in a small country like Romania. Here I compete with the whole United States."

"And you want to be a doctor?"

"I think so," he said. "But most of all I want to do medical research, like my father."

"Your father didn't come with you."

"He's dead. A long time ago, he died."

"Oh, I'm sorry."

"It does not matter. It was so long ago I can hardly remember him anymore."

"I'm curious," Alex said. "How come you're not into gymnastics, like your mother?"

"I have never been interested in gymnastics," Danut said. "And from the beginning I think my mother, she knew I was not good at it. I enjoy to watch the performers. I have lived with having the gymnasts around all my life. But my books are always coming first with me. My mother understands that. That is the kind of person she is."

Alex couldn't quite believe his last statement, but then, maybe Mrs. Lescu had a different attitude toward members of her own family than she did toward the kids she was coaching.

"Well," Alex said, "I guess I'd better get to work on my math."

She opened her book, and Danut went back to flipping through his.

After about ten minutes a warning bell rang for the first class and other kids started to drift into the room.

Alex noticed that almost everyone who walked in and saw Danut stopped for a second and stared. He was something of a shock to them, she figured, particularly in a roomful of kids wearing blue jeans, T-shirts, and sweats.

He seemed a little nervous—fussing with his books and not looking up at all. Alex felt sorry for him. And on top of everything no one took either the seat in front of him or the seat behind him. It was as though he were being isolated from the rest of the class like some kind of germ cell, she thought.

After a few minutes the math teacher, Mr. Edwards, came in and plunked his books down on his desk. When the bell rang, he said simply, "I guess you've all noticed our new student. This is Danut Lescu, son of Cristina Lescu, the new gymnastics coach. I hope you'll all give him a warm welcome."

After that it was nothing but sines and cosines. Out of the corner of her eye Alex could see Danut taking notes furiously during Mr. Edwards's lecture. Once, when she looked up from her papers, he looked up from his, too, and he smiled at her.

After class, as everyone was filing out, Mike stopped by her desk. "Care to have lunch with me today?" he asked her as she gathered up her books.

"Yeah, I'd really like to do that. I haven't seen much of you for the past few days."

Danut had gotten his books—all of them for all his classes—into one big pile by then and was headed out through the door, when a couple of girls who were having an ardent conversation bumped into him.

Danut dropped most of the books, and the loud thump made everyone look toward the door. "So sorry," he said. "I was clumsy."

The girls helped him pick up his books, giggling all the while to one another.

"What a geek that guy is!" Mike said.

"Shh, Mike, he's going to hear you," Alex snapped.

"So what? He hardly even speaks English."

"That's not true. He practically speaks it as well as you or I, except for a little accent."

"What is this?" Mike asked. "You sure you want to eat lunch with me, or would you rather eat with him?"

"With you, of course."

Mike gave her one of his dazzling smiles—the likes of which must have cost his parents two thousand dollars and two years' worth of braces.

"Hey, that's better," he said. "Listen, you can't hang around with dorks like that or people are going to get the wrong impression of you."

Mike walked her to her next class. She always felt good going through the halls with him because he had a lot of status on campus. To begin with, there was his face—"a little like Robert Redford, only better," Dee always said. And then, Mike was something of a politician as well. He'd already gotten himself elected president of the junior class, and he was aiming to be team captain and president of the student body in his senior year.

As they walked along, occasionally his shoulder would brush hers, and she felt an almost electric tingle at the contact.

Of course, for him, Alex thought, there was also a certain amount of status in having her as a girlfriend. Even if no one would mistake her for a movie star, she was generally considered the best girl gymnast on campus—a shoo-in to make the U.S. team. At least, it had looked that way until Mrs. Lescu came along.

It wasn't easy to keep a romance going at Olympic High, what with the time that had to be devoted to practices and workouts and meets. But there was still some free time on weekends.

At lunch Dee and Alex found Mike sitting with a group of guys from the ski team. It was rare for them to be around campus during the winter; that was their time for competition, and they were usually on the road then. Most of their summers were spent attending classes and catching up with school.

"What a blah lunch," Dee told the group as she surveyed the salad with a side order of cottage cheese and a slice of whole-wheat bread on her tray. The cafeteria was very strict about excluding junk food and worked on special menus for each group of athletes. Gymnasts, alas, were expected to pay strict attention to weight control.

"So, how's it going with the new coach?" Mike asked.

By now Alex had told Mike the story of the closet and her first encounter with Mrs. Lescu.

"Not too hot at practice the other day," she said. "But I've got some big plans for a new routine on the balance beam, and I'm hoping that that's going to impress her. In fact, I could use a little bit of advice."

"Sure."

"I want to make this absolutely spectacular, a collection of things that you almost never see anybody do."

"Well, that should make some sort of impact on her," Mike said.

"I suppose, but I'm not just doing it for her, I'm doing it for myself too. What I mean is, this is the routine that's going to take me to the Olympics, and it's got to be really super."

She pulled the gymnastics magazine out from the pile of books she had put down on the floor and showed Mike the article about Vera Filipova.

"See," she said, "look at that dismount—a roundoff and a double back flip off the beam. I've only seen that done once or twice in this country before, and not done well, either."

"What's a roundoff?" asked Nick Ferrara, one of the skiers.

"It's sort of like a cartwheel, but both of your legs come down at the same time," Alex said. "It's a way of changing direction, of going from forward to backward.

"So how do you think I should start this thing?" she asked Mike.

"If I were you, I think I'd try a roundoff onto the board and then jump off and do a flipflop onto the beam."

"Then maybe three flipflops and a lay-out," Alex said. "I'm going to throw in a switch leap and a side leap and a double turn."

"And maybe four back handsprings," Mike said. "You're short enough, and that's pretty impressive."

"Short enough?" Nick asked.

"Well, if you're too tall," Alex said, "by the time you finish four of them, you'd run out of board. It's only sixteen feet long."

Alex checked the cafeteria clock. "Hey," she said. "It's almost twelve-thirty. We've got to get going. I can't afford to be late anymore to these practices. Mrs. Lescu is a stickler for punctuality."

Chapter Five

On the Sunday after the disastrous Saturday practice Dee, Alex, and Melissa had gotten passes from the office and had taken the bus to town to an athletic supply store where they all bought new leotards.

"I'm never going to get caught like that again," Alex said, folding up a credit card slip for a hundred and fifty dollars' worth of gear. "But my mother is going to kill me when she gets this bill."

"Well, just explain to her what an ogre this new coach is," Melissa said.

"Now wait a minute," Dee said. "If we keep thinking like that, we're never going to get along with her. We've got to give her at least a couple of weeks before we write her off completely."

Alex stared at Dee. "You've got to be kidding," she said.

On Monday, as Alex dressed in the locker room, she put on one of her new leotards, a well-fitting dark blue one with blue stripes on the sides. She felt better already. New clothes always made her feel as if she were making a fresh start.

Mrs. Lescu was waiting for the girls out in the gym. She was wearing a droopy-looking brown sweat suit and carrying her trusty clipboard. After the girls warmed up she showed them a new chart she had made up for their training activities. Weight training was going to move to an open hour they had before breakfast, and ballet would be three days a week in between sessions on the gymnastics apparatuses.

She had devised a detailed schedule of rotations so that everyone could use the various pieces of equipment. She was going to begin holding special conferences with each team member, to help them set goals for their performances. There was a sign-up sheet for that.

And she had set up new appointments for everyone to see the school's doctor, a specialist in sports medicine. She planned to attend the appointments with each student so that she could take detailed notes on their physical condition.

"She's like some kind of machine," Melissa whispered to Alex as they stood in line to sign up for their conferences. "I can't believe this."

It was a dramatic contrast with Coach Baer, Alex had to agree. Under him things had been a lot less organized and less tightly scheduled. If you came to practice and felt like working on one thing all afternoon, or one piece of equipment, he was likely to let you do whatever you wanted to do.

"Remember those days when he just decided everyone needed a break and he'd cut the whole practice short by an hour?" Alex asked wistfully. "Or the times when he sneaked boxes of cheeseburgers into the gym? Those days are gone forever."

"You know, in a way, all that wasn't such a good idea, either," Dee said.

"Well, you have to be somewhat flexible," Alex said. "It's little human things like that that sort of build up the relationship between the kids and the coach. Maybe they don't exactly measure up to Olympic standards, but it makes you feel like you and the coach are on the same side—not opponents."

"You have to admit, Alex," Dee said, "that this is an incredible schedule she's worked out. It really gives you the feeling that you're mounting this giant campaign that's going to steamroll you right into the Olympics."

"I admit it," Alex said. "But it's sure not going to make me like her any better."

When she got to the sign-up sheet, Alex put herself down for one of the earliest appointments possible, on Thursday. She wanted to see Mrs. Lescu soon. She was eager to talk about exactly what she had in mind for her balance beam routine.

Out on the floor Mrs. Lescu had put Alex and Melissa in a group that was working on the height of their aerials for floor exercises with one of the assistant coaches, Anna Licht. Dee was in a group that was working on the balance beam. They had placed the beam in a low position on the floor and surrounded it with mats so that the girls could work without worrying about falling.

Occasionally Mrs. Lescu dropped by the floor-exercise group to watch and take notes. But it seemed to Alex that she was spending most of her time by the balance beam where Dee was.

"You know," Alex told Melissa as they watched two other girls on the mats, "Dee's attitude toward this new coach is beginning to bother me. It's so goody-goody it's disgusting. I don't think I can stand many more lectures about how dynamic and organized Mrs. Lescu is."

"Shhhhh," Melissa said. "Here she comes."

The coach walked toward their group and stood and watched for several minutes as Alex and the others performed. There was more of her furious note-taking on the clipboard.

"All right, girls." She signaled with her hand for them to stop for a moment. "I think you all have much potential. But I am believing that this is one area, the height of your jumps, where it is necessary to spend a lot more time and effort. Mrs. Licht, she is going to spot for you and really work on those blocks and angles. We do it over and over again, ten thousand times if necessary, this afternoon, until you feel you make some progress."

Then Mrs. Lescu strolled back to the balance beam. A few seconds later Alex saw Dee talking to her. Then Dee went to the beam, and after she did a few dance movements, it looked to Alex as if Dee were demonstrating the dismount that Alex had been discussing with Mike earlier that afternoon at lunch—a roundoff into a double back flip.

"Hey, Alex," Melissa said, "look at what Dee's doing. Isn't that a roundoff she's trying off the beam?"

When she did the flip, Dee went into what was known as the "pit"—a hole dug in the gym floor that was filled with foam rubber and padding so that the gymnasts wouldn't hurt themselves.

"It sure looks like it, doesn't it?" Alex said. "But she's got a lot of practice ahead of her before she can stick it. I wonder what she's trying to pull?"

After a couple of tries Dee got up, and she and Mrs. Lescu had a conversation that lasted a few minutes.

When practice finally ended, Alex not only felt tired but also filled with a growing edginess.

"Great workout, wasn't it?" Dee shouted to her as they went through the gym door into the locker room. Dee was positively beaming. Her cheeks were rosy, and she looked as if she'd just come in from a brisk jog around the campus. Little wisps of blond hair had come out of her ponytail, which was tied up with a plaid ribbon, and they curled around her face in tendrils that looked as if they'd been purposely styled that way in a beauty shop.

"Yeah," was all that Alex could say at first. But by the time they reached their lockers, she was about ready to burst.

"What was that you were practicing on the beam?" she asked.

"Oh, you mean the roundoff and the back flip," Dee said, reaching into her locker to hang up her leotard and grab a towel.

Alex shut her locker and followed Dee to the showers.

"Yeah, the thing I was telling everybody about at lunch," Alex said.

Back at their lockers after showering, they continued the conversation.

"It seems a little odd to me that no sooner do I get through describing to everyone the routine I planned to put together than all of sudden you're trying to do the same thing," Alex said.

"Just because you talk about it doesn't mean it belongs to you," Dee said. "In fact, I told you the other day that I was interested in changing my routine too. And anyway, anybody in the world could try to do that movement if they wanted to, and you couldn't stop them, could you?"

"And some of your poses on the beam, even the way you put your hand on your hip that one time—even that looks like something I sometimes do," Alex went on.

"That's crazy," Dee said.

"And then on top of it all, you're always hanging around the coach," Alex went on. "Every time I look at you during practice, you're over there trying to butter her up."

"I'm not buttering her up."

"Well, what do you call it, then?"

"It's not any different from what you used to do all the time with Coach Baer. You were always hanging around him, weren't you? Monopolizing his time so that nobody else could get near him?"

"I was?"

"You said it!"

Dee, who had finished dressing by then, slammed her locker shut, leaving Alex behind, still putting on her shoes and socks.

Is that what the other kids thought it was like between her and Coach Baer? Alex wondered. Actually, when she thought about it, she realized that maybe Dee was right. The balance beam wasn't her own personal property, was it? And neither was the roundoff into the double back flip.

But she still had that nagging feeling about Dee's actions over the past few days. Dee *was* hanging around the new coach a lot more than anyone else. She was violating a sort of unwritten rule that had always existed between them as friendly rivals: Compete hard but do it all up front—no games.

Chapter Six

Dee and Alex hardly spoke for the rest of the day. When they got back to their room after dinner, Alex announced that she was going to the library to study. Dee said she preferred to stay in their room.

When Alex got back to the dorm, Dee had already turned out the light and gone to bed. Alex had to undress using only the light from the hall.

The next morning was much the same, and Alex ended up walking between most of her classes by herself or just with Melissa.

When Alex got to chemistry class, she noticed Danut again for the first time in a couple of days. The other kids still seemed to be ignoring him.

He looked so forlorn. He hadn't changed the way he dressed at all. He still came to class in shirts, ties, and baggy woolen trousers. Whatever anybody else thought didn't seem to matter to him.

He was sitting on a chemistry lab stool with no one else anywhere near him. Now that she thought about it, Alex realized she hadn't seen anyone talk to Danut in class in the past few days—except for teachers, that is.

"This is so dumb," Alex said to Melissa. "There's

nothing wrong with that kid except that he looks a little different."

"Of course, his mother's sort of weird," Melissa said.

"Yeah, imagine what it must be like to live with her on a full-time basis. We're lucky. We only have to spend a quarter of our lives with her."

On an impulse Alex took the lab stool next to Danut. Melissa sat down next to Alex. "What are you doing?" Melissa whispered to Alex.

"He doesn't bite," Alex whispered back.

A lot of other kids looked up from their own conversations to stare at them. Alex tried not to notice. What was she doing this for? she asked herself. Considering the way that she felt about Danut's mother, it didn't make much sense. Why didn't she feel the same sympathy for Cristina Lescu that she did for Danut?

Maybe it had something to do with the fact that Mrs. Lescu acted like such a Marine drill sergeant, while Danut reminded her of some sort of exotic, mysterious foreign film star. She also sympathized that a real brain like Danut had been thrust into a school full of hundreds of jocks.

Danut seemed thoroughly absorbed in something he was reading and didn't look up.

Alex leaned over to him. "Do you ever do anything except study?" she asked.

Danut looked up. Maybe he was a little startled that someone was actually trying to start a conversation with him. "You are talking to me? I am sorry," he said. "I am not studying. I am just reading a science magazine that Mr. Amundsen gave to me."

"What's it about?"

"Gene splicing and recombinant DNA and how they might be able to synthesize plant fibers someday that are stronger than steel."

"You read stuff like that all the time, don't you?" Alex said. "Just for the fun of it."

"You are laughing at me?" Danut asked.

"No, I guess I'm just trying to make you laugh."

"Do I seem too serious?"

"A little bit, I guess. But I also think you must be pretty miserable here—I mean, the way everyone ignores you. It must be horrible being stuck in a school where everyone's so totally into athletics and you're totally into developing your brain."

"I get used to it," Danut said. "Since I was born, my mother is bringing gymnasts home. That reminds me, how is my mother doing?"

Alex swallowed hard. "Pretty good, I guess. She's certainly an organizer."

"What does that mean?"

"She's good at organizing things, getting everything put into good shape."

"That sounds pretty good."

I wonder if I should tell him the truth, Alex thought, *about how I feel about his mother.*

A moment later Mike walked into the lab with a couple of other guys in tow.

He stopped short when he saw where Alex was sitting, then walked over to her. "Hey, what's with *this* again?" he said, sort of motioning with his head in the direction of Danut.

"Cut it out, Mike," Alex said.

Sometimes Mike could be downright obnoxious. He put his arm around her shoulder and leaned down close to the lab table. "You and Melissa want to move over there?" he asked, nodding in the direction of where his friends were sitting down. "We can all work together on the experiment."

"I don't think so," Alex said. "I've got to pass this course."

"Hey, what's with you?" Melissa asked. "You playing hard to get or something?"

"No," Alex said. "It's just that when Mike and his friends get together in the lab, the result is usually broken test tubes, spilled liquids, and very few results on paper. I learned a long time ago that I'm better off working alone on these things. I have a hard enough time on my own, as it is."

"You mind if I wander over there?" Melissa asked, looking longingly at the boys at the other end of the room. "No offense, Alex, it's just that they never asked me before."

"It's okay," Alex said. "I don't mind."

Not only Melissa was gravitating that way, Alex noticed. Dee had come in and taken a seat near the gymnastics crowd as well.

Suddenly she felt as if she and Danut were some sort of science experiment themselves—and that everyone else was examining them under their microscopes. She wished she hadn't gone near him. She could see Mark Gaddini looking her way, then whispering something to Mike.

Fortunately a second later, Mr. Martin, the chem teacher, came into the room and called the class to order. "We are going to work in pairs on this experiment," he told the group. "It's a toughie."

Alex felt her face getting red. *Oh, great*, she thought, *now I've got myself roped into being Danut's partner.*

Mr. Martin walked to the back of the room and dropped off a packet of materials on Alex's desk. "I'm glad you've got someone to work with, Danut," he told the boy. "Alex can help you if you don't understand some of the words. But, as a matter of fact, you can probably read English better than some people in this classroom—whom I don't care to name."

Cute, Alex thought. *Now the teacher's not only got me paired up with Danut, but he's also laughing at the rest of the class.*

The experiment called for them to bring a series of liquids to a boil and then to compute how many parts of salt were in the liquid based on the temperature at which the liquid boiled.

Normally science experiments, whether they involved dissecting baby pigs in biology or bouncing light through prisms in physics, made Alex break out in a cold sweat. But this time she sat back as Danut smoothly and confidently took out the glassware, measured liquids into beakers, and lit the Bunsen burner.

But he didn't just do it all himself. "I don't want to keep you from learning about this, Miss Hays," he said.

"Danut," Alex said, "I think you can call me *Alex*."

He had her look up equations in books and explain to him what she thought was going on.

When Alex glanced at the other side of the room, she could see a lot of liquid sloshing around in test tubes, a good deal of bumping and jostling, and not much else. At one point Mike had to go and ask Mr. Martin for some more compound. "I'm not exactly sure which one to ask for," he told the teacher, "because somehow we got the test tubes all mixed up."

Alex and Danut had finished their experiment and turned in the finished results twenty minutes before the class was supposed to end.

"Great work," Mr. Martin said as the two gave him their papers. "You're free to go whenever you want."

They walked back to their lab area and cleaned up. Danut washed the test tubes and Alex dried. "Would you care to go out to the Student Center and drink a Coke before your next class?" he asked her as he closed the door on the glass cupboard.

Alex was stunned. One friendly gesture and now he was really moving in. Wouldn't Mike have fun with that if he found out she'd gone off for a little chat over Cokes with Danut? There was no way she could go.

"No, I can't," she said. "I mean, I'm sorry. I really should stick around and look over my English notes here at my desk while I wait for the other kids to finish. I mean, it's awfully nice of you to ask me, but I've really got to study a little bit."

"That's okay," Danut said, untying his lab apron and folding it up. "We do it maybe some other time."

He picked up his books and left the classroom.

Alex didn't know whether to feel relieved that he was gone or sad that she hadn't gone with him. She got out her literature book and tried to study, but she couldn't concentrate on the words. Why was she getting so friendly with Danut all of a sudden? It must be some kind of motherly instinct. She just wanted to help him adjust to life in this country, to find a little niche for himself.

Melissa wandered back to Alex's lab table. The braid on the back of her head was askew, and the bottoms of her jeans were soaked with water that someone had spilled on her. She had a messy, water-spotted piece of graph paper in her hand. "You were right not to sit with Mike and the guys," she said. "They've totally botched it up. We're never going to finish. I wish I'd stayed back here. That Danut really knew what he was doing."

"Yeah, he sure was good at it," Alex said.

See, she told herself, people *can* get to like him. Melissa was already beginning to recognize Danut's good qualities.

After class Mike headed straight for Alex. "Hey, Alexandra, my love," he said. "I've had it up to here with that Danube, or whatever his name is. What the heck is going on between you two? What's the story, babe?"

"There's no story," Alex said. "I just kind of thought he could use a friend."

"Well, I thought you and I—we were supposed to be going together."

"So did I."

"You sure didn't act like it today. Sitting back here and choosing him as your partner—ignoring everybody else."

"I'm sorry," Alex said. "I never thought it would end up that way. I guess I just sort of sympathize with the kid—you know, coming to a new country, trying to adjust to a totally different way of life, and nobody even paying any attention to him."

"I think he's adjusting just great. He's probably going to get an *A* in this class, and the rest of us will be lucky if we pass."

"Yeah, I bet you're right about that."

"So why don't you just lay off?" Mike said. "Leave the guy alone."

"You've got it all wrong," Alex said. "All I do is talk to him once in a while. We don't have anything in common—not like you and me. We both do gymnastics. About all he has to do with gymnastics is the fact that his mother makes her living by teaching it."

"Well, that sounds like a good enough reason to stay away from him."

Chapter Seven

On Thursday afternoon Alex showed up fifteen minutes early for her conference with Mrs. Lescu. The door to the office was closed when she got there; someone was obviously inside with the coach, even though the conference schedule that was posted on the door didn't show that there were any other appointments at that time.

Alex could hear talking and laughter coming from inside the office. After about ten minutes she wondered if she should knock and let Mrs. Lescu know that she was there. On the other hand, she figured, if she did that, she might get the coach all uptight again. No, the best thing to do was just to be patient and wait for the door to open.

While she waited she went over the notes she had written down about her routines—and in particular the ones about her hopes for developing something really spectacular for the balance beam. She wanted to sell the coach on this, really impress her with her enthusiasm and ability.

She took a couple of deep breaths and tried to concentrate on thinking positively, on picturing herself as a success—the way she always did before she went into a big meet.

Two minutes after her conference was supposed

to have started, the door opened and Dee walked out. "Hello, Alex," Dee said.

Alex gritted her teeth and felt a knot forming in her stomach. Why was it that lately Dee always seemed to get in her way whenever she wanted to approach the new coach?

"I didn't know you had an appointment this afternoon," Alex said. Making more points with the coach? she felt like adding.

"I just dropped by to talk," Dee said. "See you later."

Not if I can help it, Alex thought.

The truth was that during the past few days Alex and Dee, as much as possible, had avoided each other, which was not easy, since they were roommates. They went to meals with other friends from the dorm; they studied in different places; they got into separate practice groups in the gym.

Of course, inevitably they still did bump into each other in their room early in the morning or late at night. But they had only the most perfunctory things to say to each other.

Meeting Dee so unexpectedly at Mrs. Lescu's office threw Alex off kilter. So much depended on this interview, she said to herself, and now here she was feeling ill at ease and uncomfortable again in the coach's presence.

"Good morning, Miss Hays," Mrs. Lescu said. "I think that now we know each other a little better, perhaps we start calling each other by first names. I'm Cristina, you're Alex. Yes?"

"Yes, okay," Alex said. Her mouth felt dry; her mind went blank. She had the feeling that she should say something casual and charming, but she just couldn't speak.

"Let me begin, Alex, by saying that you are very talented gymnast," Mrs. Lescu said.

Alex felt a little spark of hope ignite inside her.

"You show lot of originality, lot of vigor in your performances. But also you are very sloppy," Mrs. Lescu continued. "And when under pressure, you crumble a little bit. Not completely falling apart; for that you are too good. But the edges, they are a little rough."

"Mrs. Lescu—I mean, Cristina—I don't see how you can say that," Alex said in a shaky voice. "I'm an elite women's gymnast, one of the best in the nation. At my last two invitationals I took lots of first places. When they wrote me up in the papers, they used words like *smooth* and *polished* to describe my performances."

"Not to believe everything you read, Alex. In fact, you—you be better off not to read it at all, win or lose."

"You make me sound as though I'm sort of mediocre or something."

"That is not at all what I said. Please to listen. I just believe you are needing to work very, very hard in next few months so that you will be ready by the time you get to the Nationals and U.S. championships. You do not want all your dreams to end before you even make it to championships. You need much intensive drill, to go over and over and over again on your weak spots so that you can perform like a machine."

"You mean, you don't think I could make the Olympic team?"

"Right now I am not so sure. If trials were held today, it would be like rolling the dice. But you have plenty of time to prepare, and then we'll see."

Coaches are not supposed act like this, Alex told herself. They're supposed to tell you how wonderful you are. They're supposed to urge you on and tell you to shoot as high as you can, just as Coach Baer used to do.

Alex sighed and pulled her papers out of her folder. "I brought some notes along about things I wanted to discuss with you," Alex said. "But now I'm not so sure. They're changes I want to make in my routines. New movements I want to try. I'm particularly interested in doing something spectacular on the beam. That's always been my best piece of equipment, and I really think that that's where I should put my gold-medal effort."

"Is now a little early to talk about gold medals, do you not think?"

"You're probably right, but I've always believed in aiming as high as I could."

Alex went over the maneuvers she had planned out on paper, explaining exactly which movements she would like to do on the beam.

"All very good—nice," Mrs. Lescu said. "I see you have put much thought into this. I do not mind you try to work on some of these things. But to do them you must concentrate on making every jump, every turn absolutely perfect. Maybe you think I make you move along more slowly than you ought to go. But I want you should be more polished, more smooth."

"Like Dee, you mean," Alex said.

"Dee? I was not thinking of Dee especially. But, yes, Dee is very smooth and polished already. Other things she needs to work on," Mrs. Lescu said.

Like not stealing my ideas, Alex thought to herself.

Mrs. Lescu stood up, signaling the end of the conference. "So now we know little more about each other," she said. "Now we get to work."

As Alex left the office she felt as if she were reaching the boiling point inside. Cristina Lescu was wrong about her. She wasn't about to crumble like some dainty little cookie. She was strong, powerful, and she was going to beat everybody at the Nationals, the championships, *and* the Olympic trials. Then, as she walked off onto the campus, she had a vision of herself on the Olympic platform, four gold medals hanging around her neck on beautiful ribbons. Little girls were handing her bouquets of flowers, and she was waving to the crowd while flashbulbs popped all around her. Mrs. Lescu and Dee were standing on the sidelines. The coach had a grim smile on her face. Dee was crying.

She would show them. She wasn't going to let Dee Winters or Cristina Lescu stand in her way.

Chapter Eight

From then on there was a change in the practice routines of the gymnastics team. It seemed to Alex that Mrs. Lescu was making her do the simplest things of all over and over again, hundreds of times, while other girls got to work with her creatively and put together more complicated maneuvers.

Sometimes Mrs. Lescu even had the whole group that Alex was working with move on to other apparatus while Alex was left behind working on some petty detail of a basic aerial jump in the floor exercises, a catch on the uneven bars, or a turn on the beam that she felt she could have done in her sleep.

Dee, meanwhile, was forging ahead and trying some dramatic new maneuvers that they had seen done at advanced meets—movements that could earn a performer a lot of risk points in competition and lead to a medal. For example, Mrs. Lescu was teaching Dee to do a flipflop onto the board in front of the vault and then to try a Tsukahara or twisting somersault off the vault.

Not that she was exactly able to do it right yet, Alex noticed with some pleasure.

The problem for Alex was that because of all the extra drill on the basics that Mrs. Lescu was forcing on her, she had little or no time left to practice the new routine that she was trying to work out on the beam.

Finally Alex exploded. "This is ridiculous!" she told Mrs. Lescu heatedly one day when she had sent her back to the mat to repeat a flip for what seemed like the thousandth time. "Most coaches push their kids all the time to try riskier and riskier things, and here you're doing everything you can to hold me back."

"There is plenty of time for pushing," Mrs. Lescu said. "Right now what you need is to go back and correct some of the errors that you built into your performance before. Then we work on the fireworks! Do not worry. It will not be long now."

One afternoon Mrs. Lescu finally allowed Alex some time to sit down with the team's choreographer and work out a few artistic refinements for her routines on the beam and in the floor exercises.

That's when Alex got the brainstorm for what she needed to do next.

She talked to Mike and Melissa about it at lunch the next day. Mike was sitting with a group of guys from the gymnastics team when she and Melissa brought their lunch trays over to his table.

"Are things going any better with Mrs. Lescu?" he asked.

"Not really," Alex said. "She's really turning me into a workhorse—making me slave away at the basics. She thinks I'm a little sloppy."

"Sloppy!" Mike said. "Doesn't this old bag read the papers? Doesn't she know how you raked in those trophies at your last couple of meets?"

"I already tried to tell her all that. It just

doesn't seem to make any difference. My big problem now is that I'm dying to work on that routine on the beam we were talking about, and I just don't have the time. She won't give me any space. So now I figured out a way that I can make time."

"What's that?" Melissa asked.

"I'm going to go down to the gym after dinner a couple of nights a week and set up the low beam and do it myself."

"You can't do it all alone," Mike said.

"You're right, I can't, so you're going to come with me."

"Uh-oh, Mike, I guess you've got your work cut out for you," Mark Gaddini said.

"Oh, no," Mike said. "I can't hack that. Get Melissa to help you."

"She's going to come, too, but she's not strong enough to do it by herself. I need somebody big—like you—to spot me and to tell me what I'm doing wrong—and to help set things up."

"What about Dee?" Mike asked.

"Forget Dee. We're having a few problems lately."

"I can't. I have too much homework to catch up on," Mike said.

"Hey, man, you and I both know that you almost never study," Alex said. "You've got to help me. Melissa, you'll do it, won't you?"

"I guess so."

"This is just a couple of nights a week we're talking about," Alex said to Mike. "Just until I get started."

"But what about the gym?" Mike asked. "Won't it be all locked up?"

"I checked that out. The janitor says it's open,

and he doesn't care, just so we don't make a mess."

"Maybe you'll just end up getting the coach upset," Mike went on.

"Who's going to get mad at somebody for working harder?" Alex asked.

"Well, okay—I'm willing to try it for a couple of nights," Mike said. "But only for an hour or two. And if I get sick of it, that's it. I quit."

"Okay," Alex said. "That's cool. We'll give it a try."

After dinner that night Alex raced up to her room to put on her leotard and a warm-up suit before Dee could get back from the cafeteria and catch her. She wasn't in the mood to answer any questions about what she was up to.

She and Melissa got to the gym first. Alex started to do some warm-up exercises while keeping her eye on the clock. First she ran around the gym, then she did a few stretches. Getting down in a crouched position, she started straightening and bending her legs, one at a time. Then lying back and supporting herself on her elbows, she rotated each leg from the hip.

"Where's Mike?" Melissa asked. "It's kind of lonely in here."

"I don't know," Alex said. "I hope he's not going to chicken out."

Finally, after about fifteen minutes, he came through the door. Alex jumped up and gave him a kiss on the cheek. "You made it," she said.

"Just barely."

Working together, they set up piles of thick, foamy crash pads around a low beam, just a couple of inches off the floor, so that Alex could get started.

"Are you sure you're ready for this?" Mike asked. "Shouldn't you start out by doing your routine on the floor?"

"I've done it a million times down there already," Alex said. "You sound like Mrs. Lescu. I'm ready to move up."

With that, Alex plunged into her routine, and they practiced for about an hour. For the first time since Cristina Lescu had arrived at Olympic High, Alex felt as if she were really accomplishing something as she smoothly rolled and flipped and turned. Occasionally she came out of an aerial a little late or too soon, and Mike had to catch her, but she felt as if she were urging her body on to do exactly what she wanted it to do.

They went over and over some of the problem moves, with Mike offering advice, until Alex couldn't do any more, and she felt weariness creeping into her muscles. "I guess I'd better stop now," she said, panting.

"Nice blocks on those last passes," Mike said. "You're really looking good, Alex—better than ever."

"I know. I mean, thanks," Alex said. "It felt so good. The height was nice on everything. The only thing is, I don't know why I can't do it that well when the coach is around."

Then she collapsed to a seated position on the gym floor and brushed back damp strands of hair from her sweat-stained face. She felt that fantastic, overall, good, tired feeling that always came to her after a solid workout.

Then Melissa spoke up. "We'd better get going," she said. "We've been here too long already, and I still have some homework to finish up for English tomorrow."

"I really appreciate the two of you coming down here tonight," Alex said. "Can we do it again Wednesday?"

"Sure," Mike said. "But only until midterms. Then we gotta break."

"Okay," Alex said. "You got a deal."

Chapter Nine

"Things still aren't going so hot for your friend Danut," Melissa told Alex when they got to chemistry class the next day.

"I wouldn't exactly call him my friend," Alex said. "But what do you mean—what happened?"

"A few guys glued his locker shut with some kind of super-sticky glue. He must have tried to do his combination about fourteen times before he finally figured out that something was wrong. Then he got the janitor and they had to pry it open with a crowbar."

"That's disgusting. Those guys are acting like a bunch of junior high school punks."

"And Mr. Amundsen is all freaked out about the locker, too, because the door was totally wrecked and bent out of shape. The school is going to have to replace it."

"I hope Mike wasn't in on that stupid prank."

"I don't think he did it, but he probably knows who did."

When Danut got to class, though, he seemed totally unflustered by the experience.

He smiled at Alex, who was sitting in the middle of a group of girls near the center of the room. She said hello but felt a little pang of guilt. Ever since that day in chemistry class when they had worked together, she had avoided any situation where she might end up sitting too close to Danut. He probably had begun to suspect that it wasn't just a matter of chance that she always seemed to get to class way ahead of him these days—and sit somewhere far away from where he would.

After class was over that day, Mr. Martin asked her to stop for a minute so he could talk to her. "Alex, I've got something I want to talk to you about," he said.

Alex went up to his desk. "You've probably noticed that things haven't been going so well for Danut since he got to Olympic High," Mr. Martin said. "That incident with the locker this morning was just the peak of the whole thing. I know he doesn't talk to his mother about what's been going on. But one of these days he will have to, and she's going to be horribly upset. You seem to be one of the few people who want to have anything to do with him, and I wondered what you think the problem is."

"I guess it's a combination of things," Alex said, feeling kind of flustered. "First of all, he's not an athlete, he's a brain. There's always friction between those types of people, even at regular high schools. But here at Olympic High—with nothing but jocks—it gets to be cosmic. On top of that Danut walks into his classes and just blows the teachers away. After struggling to teach math and science to kids like me and the other muscle brains, out of the blue they suddenly have a genius on their hands. So naturally they tend to favor him. And also, Danut really *is* different: his clothes, his accent, his manners. I guess he just stands out...."

"I think that what you say is true, but I also think that if the kids just got a chance to spend a little time with him—one on one—they might get to like him. You certainly did."

"You've got it a little wrong about me," Alex said. "I'm not really that much of a friend of Danut's. I've just talked to him a couple of times."

"But you've probably put in a thousand percent more effort than anyone else has with him. Anyway, what I was thinking was that I would like to put on a little pizza party for the kids Friday night at my house—kind of a celebration to mark the fact that we've just gotten through midterms. I'll invite maybe twenty kids or so who I think would be sympathetic to Danut, just so they can get to know him a little better. That would give him a chance to be acquainted with a few more people than he is here in class. I wouldn't tell anybody why I was doing it. I just want things to be sort of natural and casual. What do you think?"

"Maybe that would help," Alex said. Then she had an inkling of what Mr. Martin was going to say next.

"You'll come, won't you? He really could use your support."

Alex hesitated and swallowed hard. "I guess so," she said. It was probably the least she could do, she said to herself.

"Just do me a favor," Alex asked. "Don't invite Mike Schultz."

"And you do me a favor," Mr. Martin said. "Don't tell Danut I'm doing this just for him."

"Fine," Alex said.

"So it's all set. I'll start talking to everybody today."

That evening Alex went down to the library to study again. She and Dee were still keeping their distance from each other, and although Alex preferred to spend some nights studying in her room, that was becoming almost impossible because Dee was always there.

Alex walked into the main reading room at the library and saw that almost no one was there. Maybe two or three kids. But one of them was Danut—still in a tie with a navy blue V-neck sweater pulled over his white shirt. A tweed sport coat hung from the back of his chair.

How could he do it? she wondered. Why did he always want to look that way?

She sat down on a couch and stretched out her legs to rest on a coffee table. After about an hour of studying Danut walked over to her. "Care to take a break?" he asked. "Would you like to drink a Coke with me from the vending machine out in the hall?"

Alex nodded. There was no way she could get out of this one—and anyway, nobody was around to see them together this time.

"Danut, there's something I have to say. How do you manage to keep that tie on from eight in the morning until nine at night?" Alex asked as Danut pumped quarters into the vending machine.

Danut laughed.

"That's your biggest problem, you know," Alex told him. "The way you dress. It just lets all those sloppy athletes zero in on the idea they have that you're not one of them. I can't exactly figure it out, either, because I always thought all you Iron Curtain types—Romanians and Russians and East Germans and all—were wild about

American sports clothes and would pay hundreds of dollars just for a pair of jeans."

"It is true, Alex. Some of them are," Danut said. "I suppose I was just always hanging around adults more than kids—spending most of my time studying and going to school. I never had time to think so much about what I was wearing."

"Well, that's just it. You've got to start thinking about it—you've got to conform just a little bit. Mr. Martin invited you to this party he's throwing, didn't he?"

"Yes."

"Can I be frank with you, Danut?"

"Frank?"

"Really honest, I mean—without hurting your feelings?"

"Certainly." Danut smiled. "I am not an overly sensitive person, Alex."

"I know this is going to sound bad, but what I want to say is—Danut, you just can't go to that party looking the way you do."

"You don't like the color of my tie." Danut laughed.

"It's not the color of the tie, it's the tie itself! Now I'm going to be brutal," Alex said, "because there's no other way to handle this. You're too foreign-looking, too different, too mature. I don't mean to be offensive, but you're going to have to change the way you look."

"Alex, I am not sure I can change. I do not know where to start," Danut said. "You Americans—you spend a lot of time studying how you should look. I have no time for that."

Then, suddenly, it came to Alex what she had to do for Danut. It would be tricky, but when she was finished, he was going to be an all-American boy.

"Listen, I've got some extra time tomorrow afternoon," Alex said. "The coaches, including your mother, are going to a special clinic. Why don't I take you into town to buy some new clothes to wear to the party?"

"Clothes?"

"You know, some blue jeans, T-shirts. Maybe we'll even get your hair cut."

Danut shook his head. "This is crazy," he said.

"And your name. We've got to change that too. It's a nice name—it's a lot like Daniel. We'll just start calling you Dan."

"I am not sure."

"I'm not hurting your feelings, am I?"

"No. Actually, I think it's very kind of you to show concern about me."

"Do you think your mother would let you spend the money?"

"Yes."

"Then what's the problem?"

"None, I suppose."

"Okay, we've got a date, then. Tomorrow afternoon at three P.M., okay?"

"All right."

"I'll meet you—" Alex stopped, thinking for a moment. She didn't want to meet him anywhere on campus where someone might see her. "How about out at the bus stop?"

"Okay," Danut said. "We have a date."

The next afternoon Danut was out there as he had promised he would be, and the two rode down to a clothing store in town. Alex guided Danut to the men's department.

"This isn't the greatest," she said, "but it's a small town, and this is probably the best we can do."

They started fingering through the racks of men's pants. "You know your size?" she asked.

"I am not exactly sure."

"Maybe we'd better ask a clerk."

As if answering their call, a clerk charged up to them. "Can I help you?" she asked.

Alex looked up to see a teenage girl with shortly cropped hair. On one side of her head the hair was checkered, shaved into a checkerboard pattern. The other side was a tumbling mass of curls with a violet streak running across the top. She wore gray-and-white-striped pants that ended tightly at her ankles, a man-tailored vest in pink, and a violet shirt. She was chewing madly on a wad of gum.

"I guess so," Alex said. "This is a friend of mine, Danut. He's looking for some new clothes, but we're not exactly sure of his size."

The girl pulled a tape measure out of her pocket and set to work, much to Danut's discomfort. "What kind of clothes are you looking for?" she asked.

"My friend Alex thinks I need something a little more casual," Danut said.

"Man, I could go along with that," the girl said. "You look like you borrowed that outfit from Walter Cronkite. I mean, like, early sixties, and not exactly Brooks Brothers, either."

Danut laughed, but Alex felt a flush creep over her face.

"I've got a few things in mind," the girl said, "if you would let me make some suggestions."

Before Alex could stop her, the clerk had

whisked several items off the racks and sent Danut off to the dressing room. "Call me Sibyl," she told him. "You're going to love those. They'll give you a whole new look."

Ten minutes later Danut came out to show them how he looked. He was wearing a khaki-colored leather jacket with multi-zippered pockets and what looked to Alex like spotted Army camouflage pants.

"Sibyl," Danut said, "I do not think I can wear this."

"Why not?" Sibyl said. "You look stunning."

"We really want something a little more conservative," Alex said.

"Oh, no," Sibyl wailed.

"I cannot go from a suit and tie to ... this," Danut said. "I must pick something—how do you say?—in the middle."

"Right," Alex said. "Something in the middle."

"Okay," Sibyl said, throwing up her hands. "Whatever you say."

Alex walked back to the rack with Danut and together they picked out a couple of pairs of blue jeans.

After changing, Danut walked out of the dressing room to show them to her. "I am not too sure about these, either," he said.

"What do you mean, Danut—I mean, Dan. They're perfect. They look positively as American as surfboards and electric guitars."

They also picked out some corduroys and a couple of shirts as well as tennis shoes and a jacket.

"I am hoping this is enough," Danut said. "I do not know if I shall recognize myself when I look in the mirror."

"One more thing," Alex said as they came out of the store with a load of shopping bags. "We have to stop off across the street. I made an appointment for you. This might upset you a little bit, but I want you to get a haircut."

Danut laughed and ran his fingers through his hair. "Is the next stop the plastic surgeon?"

"No, there's not a thing wrong with your face, Dan."

After she'd said it, Alex was a little stunned. So was Danut, apparently, because he didn't say anything for a moment or two. Then he took her elbow as they crossed the street. He stopped her short just outside the barbershop. "I want you to know, Alex, that I do so much appreciate that you are doing this for me. You are a wonderful person," he said.

"I just hope you don't resent me manipulating you this way," Alex said. "You were just fine the way you were. It was just that I couldn't stand to see you all by yourself all the time with those crazy kids not understanding you, not getting to know you. This stuff, these clothes don't really count, you know. What counts is what's inside a person, but I was getting afraid that no one would ever find out what's inside of you."

"Thank you for taking the trouble to find out more about the inside of me," Danut said.

This was getting too heavy for Alex to handle. *Remember*, she told herself, *you're just trying to help this foreigner out a little bit.* She couldn't get too involved. She already had a boyfriend. And she tried to keep a picture of Mike's smile and his broad shoulders in front of her as they went through the barbershop door.

The haircut was really a good touch, Alex

thought as they went back to school on the bus. "Now remember," she told him, "next time you want a haircut, you've got to go back to that barber. He did a good job."

"I promise."

"One other thing you've got to promise me," Alex said. "Don't tell your mother that I was responsible for all this."

"Why? She is not going to care."

"I'm not so sure about that—me turning her studious-looking son into a sloppy-looking American teenager ..."

"My mother is a person who has tolerance."

"You've got to be kidding. That's not my experience. I mean, I don't want to criticize her to her own son, but she seems like a rigid person to me."

"You must give her more of a chance. The way that you gave one to me."

"Well, anyway," Alex said, "you promise not to tell? Just say you got tired of being the only one in class with a shirt and tie."

"I promise."

Now Danut was all set for the pizza party at Mr. Martin's house, Alex thought. After that, she wouldn't have to worry about him anymore. She'd done all that she could do for him.

Chapter Ten

That evening was the second night when Alex planned to go to the gym for extra practice. Just as they did the first time, she and Melissa went over right after dinner.

As they turned a corner on campus and neared the gym, however, Alex noticed a light coming from an upper window of the gym building.

"Look at that. The lights are on," she told Melissa.

"So what?"

"The last time we came over here it was all dark inside. I had to turn on the lights, remember?"

"The janitor must be in there cleaning up."

"I hope he doesn't kick us out because he's waxing the floor or something."

Alex pushed open the outer and then the inner doors of the gymnasium.

Inside, the room was flooded with light, and there was Dee Winters practicing a beam routine on the low balance beam, with Angela Avery watching from a nearby bleacher.

"What's going on here?" Alex asked.

Dee stopped short in the middle of a series of cartwheels and looked up. "I'm practicing. What does it look like?"

"In the middle of the night?"

"And what brings you here?"

"I came over to practice myself."

"That's what I thought," Dee said. "I heard from Mark Gaddini, that guy on the ski team, that you've been coming over here in the evenings."

"If you heard that, and you thought I came over here, then why did you show up?"

"To begin with, I didn't think you came here every night. And, besides, you don't own this gym, you know."

"That totally frosts it as far as I'm concerned, Dee," Alex said, fuming. "You'll do anything to beat me, won't you? You think that with this high-powered new coach on campus, you're going to move right in on my territory—to steal my routines—steal my practice time...."

Alex stood with her hands on her hips, trying to keep her voice at an even tone.

Dee jumped down off the balance beam and stepped toward her a couple of feet.

"Who's stealing anything from you?" Dee said, almost yelling. "This is a complete Fig Newton of your imagination."

"My imagination!" Alex was yelling now. "Is it my imagination that every time I turn around, there you are buttering up the coach? Is it my imagination that I finally get some decent practice time for myself and then you show up? Is it my imagination that I look over at you in practice, and there you are ripping off the stuff that I showed you?"

"Hey, everybody, calm down," said a voice from behind Alex. It was Mike, who had shown up late, as usual, to help spot for Alex. "What's going on here?"

"What's going on is that I came down to the

gym, and lo and behold, here's Dee, already monopolizing the equipment."

"I thought you guys were friends."

"Well, it hasn't been too friendly between us lately, let me tell you," Dee said. "She's got these paranoid ideas about me stealing the coach away from her. The trouble with Alex is that she's never had any real competition before, and now she feels me breathing down her neck, so she's getting nervous."

"So what's the big deal?" Mike said to Alex. "You came down here to practice on the beam and you find Dee, right? So all that proves is that the two of you are really motivated when it comes to gymnastics. Nothing wrong with that. Why can't both of you practice here? This is a giant gym."

"But there's only one low beam, and that's what I want to use," Dee said.

"Well, you can share it."

"I don't want to share with her"—Alex was crying now—"and I don't want you to try to negotiate this like we were two kindergarteners or something. Just stay out of it. This is between Dee and me."

Alex grabbed the door handle and pushed. She rushed out and started running down the sidewalk. In a minute Mike was beside her. "Wait a minute, Alex," he said, grabbing her arm. "I don't think this is the big crisis you make it out to be. I'm sure you can work it out with Dee without me getting involved. But for right now I think you ought to go back to the dorm and relax for a while. You're taking everything too seriously lately. Gymnastics means a lot to me, too, but you just can't get so paranoid over it. You're a fantastic gymnast, and you know it. You're tops at this school, and you're tops in the country."

"I'm not paranoid. She is pushing *me!*"

"Okay," Mike said. "So she's been bugging you lately. But let's just walk back to the dorm, okay?"

Alex nodded, and Mike put his arm around her. Would he still like her as much, she wondered, if she weren't heading for the Olympics? If he didn't think she was gold-medal material?

Mike pushed open the dorm door. "I've got an idea," he said. "There's an NCAA basketball game tonight on TV. Let's go down to the TV lounge. I thought I was going to have to miss it to practice with you. But maybe we could still catch part of it. What do you say?"

"Well, okay," she agreed, not really very interested.

A few other couples were in the lounge watching the game Mike wanted to see. That was unfortunate, Alex thought. If there had been something else on, maybe she could have had a long talk with Mike about how they felt about each other and—in particular—how she felt about gymnastics. She plopped down on a sofa and slipped off her coat.

After about an hour she decided she'd had enough. "I'm getting a little tired," she told Mike, who was sitting next to her on the sofa with his arm around her but with his eyes glued to the screen. "I think I'm going to head upstairs, maybe finish some homework before I go to bed."

Mike looked at her distractedly. "Sure," he said. "That's probably a good idea. I'll talk to you tomorrow. Don't worry about this stuff with Dee. You'll get it all fixed up."

I'll fix it up, all right, Alex thought. She knew what was going to happen next.

Alex climbed the stairs to the second-floor room she shared with Dee. The door was open, and Dee was at the dresser brushing her hair.

"Dee," Alex said when she saw her, "it just isn't working with us anymore. Do you think? Maybe I'd better switch rooms. Angela would probably come over here, then you could room with her and I could move in with Melissa. I'll talk to them about it tomorrow, if it's all right with you."

"That's fine," Dee said. "Whatever you want."

"This is really hard for me," Alex said, "but maybe it was inevitable. When two people are running neck and neck as hard as we are, they're bound to start getting on each other's nerves."

"I'm sure I don't know what you're talking about."

"Okay. You really don't know what I mean?"

"No."

"Then I guess we'd better not fight over it anymore."

Alex went to her dresser, grabbed a towel, soap, and toothbrush, and headed toward the bathroom. "I'll talk to them tomorrow," she said.

The next morning, before they had even gone to breakfast, Alex went and talked to Angela and Melissa. Melissa was wildly excited about Alex moving in, and Angela said it was okay with her. "This is so neat," Melissa said as they went out to breakfast together. "Let's get started moving you in right after practice this afternoon."

When they did get back from practice, Alex found a heap of cardboard boxes sitting on her bed in her old room. Dee was nowhere in sight.

"I wonder where she got all these?" she asked Melissa.

"The janitor probably gave them to her."

"All I know is, I want to get packed up and out of here before she gets back," Alex said.

She and Melissa set right to work tossing Alex's possessions into the cartons.

As she went through the room Alex felt a little troubled. There were the plants on the sill that they had bought together. There were three of them. Alex decided to take one and leave the other two behind. There were charts on which she and Dee had been recording their points from various meets. She was afraid to take any of that stuff down. She'd have to come back later with a piece of graph paper and make some notes, she decided. There was a stuffed teddy bear Dee had given her for Christmas the year before. She took that along.

She and Melissa and Angela made several trips back and forth with boxes, then heaved big armloads of clothes into the closets in the opposite rooms.

When it was over and Alex was sitting in her new room at her new desk, she felt oddly vacant, as if part of her were missing. The room was almost the same as far as furniture and paint and wallpaper went. But there was something missing. What was it that had happened to Dee, she wondered, that made it end up this way? She felt sad, but she was still angry too.

She had always been the best on the Olympic High gymnastics team, and she knew she was still the best. Dee wasn't going to take that away from her.

"I feel lousy," Alex said.

"I know it must be a comedown rooming with me," Melissa said. "I'm not a big star like Dee."

"Don't be dumb, Melissa," Alex said. "You're a super gymnast. Stop running yourself down all the time. I'm just upset about Dee. How could it happen that two people who were such great friends could end up this way?"

Chapter Eleven

The evening of the party, Alex and Melissa walked over to the Martins' house, which was just off campus.

"I'm sort of nervous about this," Alex told Melissa on her way over. "I hope the kids give Danut a break tonight. He's such a nice guy, and they've been giving him a hard time."

"They just have to get used to him," Melissa said. "He's new here, just like me. Believe me, I know. It takes a while to adjust."

"I hope so."

Mrs. Martin opened the door, and there was a blast of music from a stereo somewhere in the back of the house. "C'mon in," Mrs. Martin yelled over the background noise. "Alex, Melissa," she said. "I'm so glad to see you. Almost everyone's here already."

They went into the family room where about fifteen kids were sitting and talking, trying out Mr. Martin's home computer or looking through his records while the music played.

"Good grief," Melissa exclaimed, "look at Danut! He's talking to a bunch of girls."

Alex looked over and, sure enough, there was Danut, the center of a little cluster of kids. He looked her way as she came through the door and waved hello.

"And he doesn't look too bad for a change," Melissa added. "No kidding, those clothes make a big difference."

"He does look pretty good," Alex said, looking at Danut in his jeans and sweater. She only wondered why she suddenly felt more upset than happy about seeing Danut as the center of so much female attention. Wasn't this what she wanted? Wasn't he supposed to make his own friends so he didn't have to depend on her so much anymore?

Beth Schmidt broke away from the little cluster around Danut and walked up to Alex.

"What's going on over there?" Alex asked, nodding toward Danut.

"Oh, he was just telling us about school in Romania and how he knows some of the big gymnastics stars, like Nadia Comaneci."

"Did he ever tell you about her?" Melissa asked as Beth walked away.

"No," Alex said, "we didn't talk much about gymnastics."

Among the crowd around Danut were Dee and Angela, Alex noticed. That meant she would feel funny about rushing up there to talk to him herself. "I think I'm going to help Mrs. Martin out in the kitchen," Alex said.

"Just in time," Mrs. Martin said as Alex walked in the door. "Help me carry out these pizzas."

Alex grabbed a tray and carried it into the family room. It took them several trips before everything was set. Then Mr. Martin yelled for everyone to come to the table.

"What did I tell you?" Mr. Martin whispered to

Alex as she walked past. "He's doing just great. Everybody seems to be mixing pretty well. And those clothes of his are really an improvement, aren't they? I'm glad he finally started to adapt a little bit."

"Right," Alex said. "He looks cool."

"Do you think maybe after dinner we should all sit down and he could give us a little talk about Romania? Maybe have him show us things on a map?"

"I don't know," Alex said. "That seems a little bit like school or something. It looks as though he's doing just fine right now."

"I guess you're right," Mr. Martin said. "That might be pushing things too much."

As she was going through the line for pizza Alex bumped into Dee. "Hello," Alex said.

"Hello," Dee answered back.

"How's it working out with Angela?"

"Just fine."

Alex found it hard to think of anything else to say. Maybe her imagination *had* been blowing this thing between them out of proportion.

"I guess it's for the best—my moving out," she said. "At least for now."

Dee said nothing.

"Maybe later on we could get together sometime and talk about it," Alex added.

"I don't think we have anything to talk about."

Dee picked up her plate and glass and walked back to a sofa to sit next to Danut.

"She is too much," Melissa said. "Now she's following the coach's son around too."

After they'd eaten and then helped Mrs. Martin clear away the debris from the pizza, Mr.

Martin shoved the furniture out of the way, and some of the kids started to dance.

Alex walked over to the group standing around the stereo. "Most of this stuff is from the sixties," said Beth Schmidt, thumbing through the records. "But some of it isn't too bad."

Beth stopped the turntable and put three or four records on the spindle.

As the music started again Alex glanced out at the impromptu dance floor. "Look at that!" Beth said. "Now he's even learning how to dance. I can't believe my eyes."

Sure enough, Angela Avery and Dee had Danut out in the middle of the room and were showing him some dance steps as Beatles' guitar music bounced off the walls. Danut was laughing and shuffling his feet.

"You're getting it," Angela yelled above the sound. "That's great."

After about ten minutes of dancing Angela, Dee, and Danut collapsed on a couch. Angela and Dee left to get something to drink, but Alex still felt hesitant about going up to talk to Danut.

"Aren't you even going to go talk to him?" Melissa asked her. "Here you are, probably his best friend, you go to a party for him, and you don't even say a word."

"I guess you're right," Alex said, walking toward the couch.

Danut stood up as he saw her coming. "Alex," he said. "I have not had a chance to say a word to you all night."

"I know," she said. "You're the most popular guy at the party."

"I owe a lot of it to you," he said. "You sort of

gave to me a crash course in how to become an American teenager, didn't you?"

"Yeah, I guess so." Why did she feel so self-conscious? Alex wondered. He was just a friend, right? "But I didn't really do very much. You're a pretty nice person, Dan, and I'm glad those other dumb kids are finally beginning to recognize that."

"Are you going to stay for some moments? Maybe I could walk with you back to your dormitory?"

"No, I don't think so. I've got to go now, and something tells me no one wants you to leave. I'll see you in class Monday."

"Or perhaps in the library."

"Right."

Alex and Melissa got their coats and left. "Gee, you sure wanted to leave early," Melissa told her as they walked back. "What's the problem?"

"We've got to get up early for practice, don't we?"

"I guess so, but so do most of the other kids at the party."

"Well, I've got to get some sleep. I feel tired."

"It's nice to see everything working out for Danut."

"Yeah."

"All those kids . . . all those kids being nice to him. It's like I told you, once everybody gets used to having him around, they'll start to like him better."

Melissa was right. So why did it upset her that Danut suddenly had all these new friends? Alex asked herself. She should be glad, shouldn't she?

Chapter Twelve

On Monday in practice, Mrs. Lescu called for a ten-minute break in the middle of their workout and ordered everyone to go sit in the gym bleachers.

"What a relief," Alex told Melissa. "She must have had me doing that aerial in the floor exercises fifty times in a row. I feel as if my brains are scrambled, and I took a couple of bad falls too."

After everyone was seated Mrs. Lescu tapped her pen on her clipboard for silence. Immediately all conversation stopped. "She has us well trained, doesn't she?" Alex whispered to Melissa.

Mrs. Lescu glared up at her.

"I have a special announcement to make," the coach began. "This is not something that makes me happy, but I must go through with it, and I hope you be as cooperative as possible."

There were immediate groans. "I wonder what she's got in store for us now," Melissa said.

"Young ladies, please. I do not wish to talk to myself," Mrs. Lescu said. "Is not what you think. In fact, some of you will be most pleased, I am sure.

"I have just been informed by Mr. Amundsen that *Sports World* magazine will be on campus for the rest of this week. They will take photos and interview students for a cover story in magazine."

"Wow!" Melissa gasped. Across the bleachers there was a buzz as everyone started talking at once.

"I forbid this should interfere with our practice time," Mrs. Lescu went on. "In fact, I say to Mr. Amundsen it is not possible to interrupt our workouts to talk to magazine people. All interviews must be held in break times or before and after practice. That is clear?"

Fifteen girls nodded their heads.

"Wait until my mother hears about this," Melissa said. "She'll be stunned. Imagine being in a cover story in *Sports World*. But then, you're probably used to appearing in magazines and newspapers, aren't you?"

"Not exactly," Alex said. "There have been a few newspaper stories about me after I performed in some big meets. And everybody's been in their hometown paper a couple of times, I guess. But nothing like this. Nothing national."

"They're probably going to pay a lot of attention to you, Alex. I can see your picture on the cover now."

"I can't say I would mind," Alex said. "It wouldn't hurt anybody's sports career to be on the cover of *Sports World*."

Alex couldn't help sneaking a glance at Dee, sitting a few yards away from them. She wondered what she thought about the *Sports World* visit.

The next afternoon, the *Sports World* staff showed up at practice for the first time.

"Look at that," Angela Avery almost squealed when she saw them walk through the gym door. "Look at all the cameras."

One of the group was a very tall woman with long brown hair, large wire-rimmed glasses with lenses tinted a light shade of pink, and the longest nails that Alex had ever seen—painted a dark cranberry color. "She must be the reporter," Melissa said. "She's got a notebook and a tape recorder."

Then there were two men, both with large satchels and a couple of cameras hanging around their necks. Mr. Amundsen was with the little group, and he took them over to shake hands with Mrs. Lescu. The reporter was introduced as Nikki West. The photographers were Tom Spitz and Randall Bold.

"Mrs. Lescu looks nastier than ever, doesn't she?" Alex said to Melissa. "She must be trying to scare them off."

But in spite of the coach, the photographers and reporter seemed to be settling down for a long stay. They took off their gear and put it down on the bleachers and huddled together for a long talk. Then they sat down to watch.

Alex didn't want to say anything to Melissa, but she was more than mildly interested in the visit by the magazine. The past few weeks under Mrs. Lescu had been so frustrating that Alex was longing for some recognition. In spite of what the coach had said to her at her conference, she was improving, she was sure of it. She felt that her movements on all the apparatuses were becoming more accurate and sure.

Every day she had thrown herself into her routine with real determination. She had made up her mind to beat Dee; she was going to show Mrs. Lescu.

She had also kept on practicing in the evenings when she had a chance—and when she was sure that Dee wasn't going to be there.

Somehow, getting into *Sports World* would be like proving to everyone that she had arrived. It would be a little foretaste of what she hoped the future would hold.

"Watch this," she told Melissa. "I'm really going to make this sizzle."

Alex walked up to the balance beam. The timing of the reporter's visit couldn't have been better, she thought. She had been right in the middle of practicing her new routine on the beam. Now she had it just about perfect, and even Mrs. Lescu had grudgingly agreed earlier in the week that Alex was ready to move the beam up to a middle position in practice.

Basically the routine had ended up a lot like what she had worked out with Mike at lunch several weeks ago. The mount onto the beam was a roundoff on the board next to the beam followed by a flipflop or back handspring.

She then went into three flipflops and a layout. Other tumbling passes included a split leap, a kickover flipflop, a one-arm handstand, and a straddle jump. Intermixed with the tumbling were dance movements and poses she had worked out with the choreographer—graceful extensions of arms and legs that were supposed to give her routine a balletlike quality. The dismount was a roundoff followed by a double back flip off the beam.

Of course, at this point, because she was still

doing the routine on the medium-height beam, she had to do a simpler version of her mount.

Now Alex walked up to the beam, glanced in the direction of the *Sports World* people, and thought she had caught the eye of the reporter.

She raised her arms, did a roundoff, and mounted the beam perfectly. After some handsprings she did an in-the-air somersault with absolute precision. She felt that tight, exhilarating feeling that always came to her with aerials. It was a feeling of power, as if she were completely in control—as if she could do something that almost no one else in the world could do so well.

Her leaps were high and graceful with legs and arms extended. She felt herself moving with accuracy and elegance.

She went into the one-arm handstand with ease and strength. No bobbles, no wobbling. She knew she was making it look easy, even though it was something that took years to perfect. A few more movements and she did a simpler version of the dismount she had been planning and landed on her feet in exactly the right position.

"That was wonderful," Melissa told her as she walked away from the beam. "But I don't know if any of them saw it."

"You're right," Alex said, looking in the direction of the magazine reporter. "They're all looking at Dee."

They weren't just *looking* at Dee, either. They were pointing at her and obviously talking about her.

"I guess it's understandable," Alex said. "She looks even better than usual today."

"But she's not doing anything special."

"I know, but she looks great when she does it."

Dee was doing some fairly simple circles and swings on the uneven bars. Her hair was tied back in two pigtails high on her head with pale blue ribbons that exactly matched the color of her leotard. It always amazed Alex that no matter how hard Dee worked out, no matter how many flips or turns she made, after the routine was over, every hair on her head always looked perfect. The other girls' ponytails would start to come undone or their braids start to look ratty. But not Dee's.

And while everyone else on the team had to stick to cottage cheese and yogurt for lunch, Dee could have eaten Big Macs and Whoppers every day and never gained an ounce. It didn't seem fair.

Now one of the photographers had gotten up and was beginning to shoot pictures of Dee.

"Could you do that again?" he yelled at Dee.

Dee completed a flip that took her from one bar to the other and then back again.

"Once again?" he asked.

Dee obliged and then dropped down off the bars.

"Could I get your name?" the photographer asked, grabbing a pencil and a small pad of paper from his pocket.

"Dee . . . I mean, Deirdre Winters," Dee said.

Just then Mrs. Lescu walked up. "I am perfectly willing for you to take as many photos as you wish, young man. But the girls must now continue with their practice. Please try to shoot them only as they do their normal routines."

"Okay, okay," the man said, backing off. "We'll get together later, okay, Deirdre?"

He returned to the crew in the bleachers.

In all, the photographers and reporter spent about an hour watching them practice, and Alex estimated that about fifty percent of the time the photographer was taking pictures of Dee.

"Oh, Dee," Angela Avery gushed as the team went back into the locker room after practice. "They just loved you. They spent all their time simply ogling you."

"I didn't really notice," Dee said. "I was so busy practicing on the uneven bars."

"Are you really going to call yourself 'Deirdre' in *Sports World*?" Angela asked.

"I guess so," Dee said. "That's my real name, and I think my mother would like it that way. 'Dee' is so babyish."

"I'm going to throw up," Melissa muttered to Alex.

"Forget it," Alex said. "This is only the beginning. They've got a lot more to see."

For the next couple of days the trio from the magazine followed basically the same routine: They shot a few pictures of the other girls but roll after roll of Dee.

"This is getting to be too much," Melissa told Alex after the third photo session. "We ought to find out what they're up to. I thought this was supposed to be a story about Olympic High, but instead it seems to be turning into 'This Is Your Life, Dee Winters.'"

"What do you mean that we should find out what they're up to?" Alex said.

"Well, there's obviously some focus, some angle to this story, and maybe if we can find out what it is, we can make sure the rest of us get more press."

"The way this is shaping up, by the time we

get to the Olymics, Deirdre's going to be a superstar, isn't she?" Angela asked, breaking into their conversation as they sat on the bleachers during a break.

"Just picture it," Angela said. "Deirdre will be flooded with requests for endorsements—Deirdre on a box of Wheaties, Deirdre with her own line of leotards, Deirdre pushing vitamin pills."

Dierdre? Alex thought to herself. Whatever happened to her old friend Dee?

"How about Deirdre doing cartwheels and handstands and Tsukaharas off the vault? Or won't she have time for that?" Alex asked.

"Well, obviously that comes first," Angela said. "We all know how you feel about Deirdre these days. You're really feeling the pressure. You know that she's going to give you a tough time at the Nationals, and you're jealous because of all the attention she's getting."

"Get lost, Angela," Alex said. "Being in a magazine doesn't have anything to do with whether you win or lose. I couldn't care less about this *Sports World* garbage."

"I'll bet," said Angela, standing up and climbing to another bleacher several yards away.

But the more Alex thought about it, the more she realized she did care about *Sports World*.

"I changed my mind," Alex said to Melissa. "Let's find out what's going on with this article—just like you said."

Chapter Thirteen

"Just exactly how do you think you're going to accomplish this?" Melissa asked.

"Maybe we should try to get one of those photographers alone and ask him a few questions about what's going on," Alex said.

The two of them were in their dorm room that night, along with Beth Schmidt from the team.

"Or maybe," said Alex, "we should keep an eye on that reporter and see what we can get out of her."

"I already know something," Beth said. "They've been concentrating on one or two girls on each of the teams—swimming, track, whatever. And they haven't paid any attention to the boys' teams at all. It's beginning to look as if they're zeroing in on women's athletics."

"They all show up every afternoon at about twelve-thirty," Alex said, "and they always drop by the cafeteria first. I think Mr. Amundsen serves lunch to them in his private dining room. How about if we wait around for them there? It'd be a good chance to get them alone."

"I don't know," Melissa said. "It kind of scares me. I mean, what would I ask them?"

"Great, Melissa," Alex said, "and you were the

one who kept telling me we had to find out the angle for this story."

"I'm sorry."

"Well, at least meet me at twelve-thirty outside the cafeteria," Alex said, "and we can decide where we'll go from there on."

"Okay," Melissa said grudgingly.

Alex started waiting the next afternoon at twelve-twenty. No Melissa. At twelve-twenty-five a car rolled up with the reporter and photographers inside. Still no Melissa.

The trio from *Sports World* walked into the cafeteria and then down the hall toward the private dining room. Alex followed them in the door and hung around at the end of the hallway. She saw the three go into a coatroom and drop off their gear.

"Boo," somebody said next to Alex.

"Melissa, you are such a jerk! You practically scared me to death," Alex said. "Come on. We've got to hurry. I just saw them go in the coatroom, and I think maybe they left some briefcases behind. I want to go in there and look around."

"You can't do that! It's probably against the law or something. It would be like interfering with freedom of the press."

"Yeah, I understand there's a new amendment to the Constitution—Congress shall allow nobody to look at a reporter's notes."

"Is that what you're planning to do? Look at her notes?"

"I don't know. I just know I'm not going to let Dee get into *Sports World* that easily. What I want you to do is stand outside the coatroom door and let me know if anybody comes along."

"That's crazy."

"C'mon."

"I'm too scared. I mean, what will I say if anybody does come along and wants to go in there?"

"You'll think of something."

Alex slipped down the hall and went into the coatroom. Melissa followed.

Alex had just spotted what she thought were some briefcases when Melissa popped her head into the coatroom. "Somebody's coming."

Alex walked out the coatroom door, and the two of them met one of the photographers head-on.

"Hey," the man said, "what's going on here?"

"We're waiting for somebody."

The man seemed to accept their answer and nodded his head. He went into the coatroom to get some cigarettes out of a pocket.

"Say," Alex said as he came back into the hallway, "aren't you one of those photographers from *Sports World*?"

"You got it," he said.

"I guess we're all wondering how this article is going to turn out. I mean, what's the angle for the story, anyhow? Who's going to be in it?"

"Wouldn't you like to know?"

"Come on," Alex said, "what's the big secret? We're all going to find out in a couple of weeks, aren't we?"

"It's no big secret," he said. "It's just that it's supposed to be a pleasant surprise. What I mean is, if we told certain people now that they were going to be in the article, and then we changed our minds later, they might get upset."

"Well, it looks to everybody as if all you ever take pictures of on campus is girls—and the best-looking girls on top of it," Alex said. "Are we jumping to conclusions or are we guessing right?"

"That's a pretty good guess," the man said. "What you're going to see in *Sports World* next month is going to knock the swimsuit issue that *Sports Illustrated* put out right off the newsstands. It's going to be a hot seller, let me tell you."

"That's really something," Alex said.

"Listen, kids," the photographer said as he pulled open the door of the private dining room. "You'd better not spread that around campus, because nothing's set in concrete yet. Like I said, some people might be disappointed if they thought they were going to make it and then they didn't."

"So it's what we all thought," Melissa said. "They are zeroing in on so-called beautiful girls. It doesn't have much to do with talent, does it?"

"But he did say it's not all over yet," Alex said. "Maybe there's still something we can do about it."

Chapter Fourteen

"All we really have to do," Alex told Melissa that afternoon as they went in to practice, "is get together with these people and convince them that they ought to take gymnastics a little more into account in this article. It doesn't make any sense to come to a high school like this and zero in on faces."

"I don't know about that," Melissa said. "First of all, most of the people they've picked out aren't exactly lacking in talent. Dee's a pretty good gymnast, after all. And look at Crystal Delehanty on the swim team. They don't call her the Golden Girl for nothing. And second, they're never going to change their minds about how they want to do this article now. It's too late."

"So there's nothing we can do about it?"

"I didn't say that," Melissa replied thoughtfully. "Actually, there may be something you can do about it. Why don't you make an appointment to see that reporter alone sometime? Maybe back here in the gym. Maybe you can convince her that you're just as glamorous as Dee."

"Me, glamorous?"

"You're not exactly ugly," Melissa said. "You could get all fixed up in advance and put on a special performance for her. Maybe you could have your hair done and get Beth to help you put some makeup on."

"Makeup? Nothing but lipstick has ever touched this face."

"I'll let you borrow my new leotard—the coral-colored one with the white stripes. It would be perfect with your hair."

"What good would that do?"

"Then you could do a couple of your routines, and maybe if they saw how good you were and how nice you looked, they'd use you instead of Dee in the article."

"I don't know about that. I'd like to be in it, but it really shouldn't be the focus of my life to get clippings, should it? And anyway, there are lots of girls on the team who deserve to get into the article too. Why should it be me any more than them?"

"Because you have the best chance, that's why! If they really watched you do that routine of yours on the high beam, it would blow them away."

"I've never done it on the high beam before."

"You can do it. You said yourself that Mrs. Lescu has been holding you back."

"I guess so."

"Listen," Melissa said, "you've got to do it. Dee was almost impossible to be around before. Now she's getting unbearable."

"I'll think about it," Alex said.

As they went through the door and into the gymnasium, Alex spotted Dee up on the bleachers with the reporter, Nikki West. Nikki seemed to be taking notes while Dee talked.

As the rest of the team filed in, followed by Mrs. Lescu, Dee came bounding down the bleachers to join them. She passed by Alex and almost seemed to swing her ponytail in Alex's face. "All this stardom," she said to Alex. "I can't stand it."

Alex walked up to Melissa. "I'm going to do it," she said through clenched teeth. "I'm going after that reporter."

During a practice break Alex went looking for the reporter, whom she found in the locker room where she was flipping through her notes and reading a book of Olympic statistics.

"Hi," Alex said. "That an interesting book you're reading?"

"Just checking a few things," the reporter said.

"I'm Alex Hays."

The reporter looked up again. "Hello, Alex, I'm Nikki West."

"I already know your name. Everybody knows who you are. We're all really excited about your visiting the school and everything."

"Right."

"Could I talk to you for a minute?"

"Aren't you supposed to be out there practicing or something?"

"We're having a break right now."

"Oh."

"Just for a minute."

"Sure. Why don't you sit down and tell me what it's all about."

Alex sat down on the bench and took a deep breath. "It's this way," she said. "A couple of us thought that maybe you'd like a little demonstration of what it's really like during our performances. Something with a little more tension and pressure to it."

"Well, I think I've gotten an eyeful here during the past few days. I can tell a roundoff from a cartwheel now, and a Yamashite from a Tsukahara. And just about everything I brought along is covered with chalk. I think I've got lung damage from breathing the stuff for two or three hours a day."

"Yeah, we do use a lot of chalk on our hands and everything."

"So I'm not exactly sure what could be gained by seeing anything else right now."

"Yeah, but when we're out there at practices, it's a little more casual, a little more relaxed. People are liable to take a break in the middle of one of their routines or drop something if they muff it. What I wanted to do was to really show you what it was like as if we were in the middle of a meet."

The reporter sighed.

"I know you're getting a little tired of it. But reporters are supposed to be ready to go that one extra mile to get a story, aren't they? They're supposed to be ready to dig and really investigate before they do a story."

"This isn't exactly the Watergate conspiracy."

"You'll do it, won't you?"

"Okay," Nikki West said. "One last shot. But I can only give you about twenty minutes. Let's say I meet you back here at the gym tonight at eight. We can do that, can't we? They'll let us in?"

"Sure, sure," Alex said. "I'll take care of everything."

"It's all set," Alex said after she had raced back to the gym and found Melissa. "For eight tonight. Now we've got to get to work."

After practice Alex and Melissa decided to skip dinner. Melissa did race over to the cafeteria, though, and grab a couple of apples and oranges to sustain them.

Beth Schmidt, whose mother was a hairdresser, volunteered to come down and do Alex's hair. After Alex washed it Beth set to work with a blow dryer and curling iron. She sprayed it afterward until it felt like a rock to Alex. "Nothing's going to move those curls now," Beth said, patting Alex's hair one final time.

Melissa and Beth both got together to put on Alex's makeup. First a light dusting of powder. "I've never worn it before in my life," Alex said.

Then a touch of violet eye shadow, eyeliner, and false eyelashes that Beth had borrowed from her roommate.

"I don't know how I'm ever going to be able to see to do my routines with these things on," Alex said, fluttering her lids in the mirror. "They certainly are dramatic, though."

Then she put on Melissa's leotard and, as a final touch, coral lipstick that Beth had dug up, which was exactly the color of the leotard, and coral nail polish.

"Dynamite," Beth said, and whistled as Alex spun around for a final inspection.

"You'd make a super magazine cover," Melissa said.

"You just need one more thing," Beth said.

"What's that?"

"Hang on a minute." Beth raced out the door and back to her room.

She came back with two little white nylon-covered pads. "These are to put inside your bra," she said.

"I can't do that," Alex said. "That's where I draw the line."

"You have to," Beth said. "You just don't look sexy enough. Don't be afraid. They're very discreet—I wear them all the time, myself. You're not going to flop around or anything. You'll just look more . . . seductive. Less like a little girl."

Beth handed them to Alex, and Alex stuffed them in. "See?" Beth said, pushing Alex toward the mirror. "No one would ever guess."

"I guess it's all right," Alex said.

"It's wonderful," Melissa said. "The perfect touch."

"Now don't mess up your hair when you go outside," Beth said. "I brought this scarf for you to put on. But don't tie it on too tight, either."

Alex put on her warm-up suit and a jacket over that and tied on the scarf. She felt unnaturally padded and stuffed and glued together. "If I smile, I think my face is going to crack," she said.

They got to the gym at about seven forty-five, flipped on the lights, and Alex started to warm up. "You're really going to do this on the competition beam?" Melissa asked.

"I have to," Alex said. "There isn't much point in asking her to come over here if all I'm going to do is something she's already seen in practice."

"You're sure you're ready?"

"Don't worry," Alex said. "I can do it."

After a few laps around the gym and some stretching exercises, Alex started to get nervous.

"I hope these eyelashes don't fall off before she gets here," Alex said.

"Just keep warming up. She's got another five minutes," Melissa said.

Alex got back to work. "It's five after eight,"

she said a little while later. "I hope I didn't get into this costume for nothing."

A few seconds later Nikki West burst into the gym. She was wearing a fur-trimmed raincoat now, and she had the hood up. "Boy, it's cold out there," she said. "I can't believe I went out in this kind of weather for this."

"Hello," Alex said. "We're really glad you could come. We won't waste your time."

Nikki West took one look at Alex and stepped back, blinking for a second. "Wow," she said, "you really look different."

"I just wanted you to get some idea of what it's like in competition."

"You really make up that way?"

"Well, under the lights and everything, it's a lot like being on stage or something."

"I see."

"We'll just set up a few things here," Alex said, "and then I'll get started. It's just going to take a minute, and we won't waste any of your time."

"That's okay," Nikki West said. "You've got twenty minutes. Actually, I could probably squeeze out half an hour."

Melissa and Alex started maneuvering a few mats into place and checked the position and setting of the balance beam. "She's really impressed with you," Melissa said. "I can tell."

"I hope so."

Alex took a stand slightly behind one of the balance beams, closed her eyes, and thought through her routine. She pictured herself rounding off onto the board and then doing the backward flips that came after. The mount was one of the most important parts of the routine, and she wanted it perfect. And she didn't just want it to be wildly acrobatic, either. She wanted to be smooth and elegant, the way Dee could do it.

"Now!" she whispered to herself. She opened her eyes and took off.

Her mount was perfect, and so were her flips, and from then on, the next minutes moved smoothly forward like a dream. She kept her body tightly in control, in a centered balance over the middle of the thin little padded board. Her underwear, the strange leotard, the sticky, heavy feeling on her eyelids—she tried to wipe all of them out of her mind. She was doing it.

Finally it was almost over, and she was ready for her dismount. It worked. A double back flip and she was on the mat with her feet in perfect position. She had hit it just right. Her hands went up in the air.

Nikki West stood up and clapped for Alex. "Terrific," she said, but she let out a little giggle and covered her mouth as if she were trying to smile. "That was wonderful. You're going to do very well in competition. Even I can tell that. You've got a little problem with that outfit, though. I wouldn't wear that when I competed if I were you."

Alex looked down at the leotard and discovered that both falsies had slipped down under her bra and were lying in lumps across her stomach under the skintight fabric. "Oh, gosh," she said, trying to slide them with her hands back up under her bra.

Melissa looked horrified. Her mouth and eyes were wide-open.

"I guess I overdid it a little bit with this," Alex said. "I was just trying to look a little more attractive or something. It wasn't my idea, and I guess it wasn't a very good idea, either."

"I'm sorry," Nikki West said, walking over to Alex and putting her arm around Alex's shoulders. "I shouldn't laugh. If you saw me up there on that beam, that would be a real joke."

Nikki West looked at her watch. "Well, I think I'd better be going now," she said. "I really appreciate the effort you've put into this, and I'm sure it will help me with my article."

"But," Alex said, "I don't think you're getting the point."

"What point?"

"The reason we did all this."

"And what was that?"

"Well, I'm going to come out and say it straight. We heard that you were planning some kind of article with beautiful girls to represent each of the sports teams on campus."

"You did?" Nikki's lips tightened into a straight line.

"It was pretty obvious, wasn't it?" Alex said. "You kind of hung around girls like that all the time, didn't you?"

"I guess it looked like that," Nikki said. "But there's more to it than that."

"Are you or aren't you doing a story like that?"

"All right, we are. So now what?"

"Well." Alex took a deep breath. She didn't know if she could come out and say it or not. "I guess the reason I did all this is that I wanted to be considered as one of those girls. I was trying to make myself more glamorous. But I also wanted to show you that you don't have to sacrifice performance for glamour, either. You can have both, right? I suppose I didn't do that great a job of demonstrating all that to you."

"I admire your determination," Nikki said. "And this is kind of embarrassing, you finding all this out and trying to impress us. But the fact is, the article is pretty well worked out now. We took a lot of photos. We sent the contact sheets back to New York. And an editor there picked the girls already. Now everybody's been interviewed and we have almost all the shots we need."

"So what you're telling me is that it's too late, anyway."

"Yes, that's what I'm telling you. So I guess I'd better be going now. There's really nothing more I can do for you."

Nikki West picked up her purse and started buttoning her coat.

"I think you know who from the gymnastics team is going to be featured, anyway," Nikki said.

"I know."

"It's Deirdre," Nikki went on. "I hope there's no hard feelings about this. It wasn't that we wanted to pick somebody based on their ability or anything. You ought to keep that in mind. It was strictly the face and the body."

"That's ridiculous," Alex said.

"Don't be angry," Nikki said. "I'm sure you're going to have a wonderful career in gymnastics, and somewhere along the way somebody's going to do a big story on you too. I'll probably see you again at the Olympics."

"I hope so," Alex said.

Nikki was out the door, and there was nothing left for Melissa and Alex to do but put their coats on, turn out the lights, and go back to the dorm.

"Don't be too depressed, Alex," Melissa said. "You were fantastic on the beam, you really were. Nobody can take that away from you. You've really changed since the new coach got here. You're just getting better and better."

Alex pulled the two falsies out of her bra. "This was really a bad idea," she said.

"Yeah," Melissa said. "What a flop."

Chapter Fifteen

It was three weeks later when the copies of *Sports World* with Dee on the cover hit the campus.

"Here's the bad news," Melissa said, walking into their room with a copy under her arm one evening after dinner. "They just delivered a whole pile of these to every dorm on campus."

"For free?"

"No way. They're selling them down at the front desk for two dollars, but even so, kids were buying them like mad."

"She really does look fantastic," Alex conceded, looking at the cover.

Dee had been photographed in a split leap on the beam—arms outstretched, legs split—like a bird in flight. Her face was radiant, lit by a giant smile. She was wearing her red, white, and blue team suit and tiny white gym slippers.

"Did you see them shoot this one?" Melissa asked. "I didn't know she could get that high. She looks as if she's ten feet in the air or something."

"I think it's just something they do with the camera lenses to make it look like that," Alex said.

"You're probably right."

Alex leafed through the magazine to the story

while Melissa looked over her shoulder. Just as she and Melissa had expected, there were profiles of six top girl athletes on campus—each of them stunning. But Dee was clearly the star. She was the obvious first choice for the cover.

"Hey, your name is mentioned in there, and so is Beth Schmidt's," Melissa said. "That's not much consolation, but at least it's something. That reporter must have been impressed with your routine that night."

"I don't think so," Alex said. "She probably would have put me in there, anyway. She must have gotten the name from Mr. Amundsen."

"Read what it says about Dee," Melissa said. " 'Her coach, Cristina Lescu, says that Deirdre Winters may not be the most flashy and daring gymnast on the team, but she does have the most smooth and elegant execution.' You think Mrs. Lescu actually said that?"

"I don't know. She didn't like those reporters much, but I suspect that's what she actually thinks."

"What's wrong with your execution?"

"She thinks I have some rough spots," Alex said. "But I've been working on them, I really have."

"What an idiot that coach is," Melissa said. "All she ever does is come over and yell at you all the time."

"I just got off to a bad start with her, I guess. I've never been able to overcome that bad first impression she got of me."

Alex sighed and tossed the magazine on the bed. "It's not that I care that much about the article," she said. "It's just the latest depressing thing in a whole string of depressing things. I'm turning into an also-ran. Maybe I should get out of this place."

"What place?"

"Olympic High. Maybe I should go home."

"Are you kidding? And give up gymnastics?"

"No, just go home and train with some private coach."

"You can't do that, Alex. You're one of the future hopes for American gymnastics."

"Not according to Mrs. Lescu and *Sports World*."

"Don't listen to them. You've got to hang in there. You can't quit now."

"Well, I'm thinking about it."

"So think about it some more. Don't do anything dumb."

"We'll see."

Alex flopped down on her bed and buried her face in her pillow. "You know what's really going to be horrible?" Alex said, lifting her head up from the pillow.

"What?"

"Listening to Angela Avery and Dee gloat over this whole thing."

"You're right about that," Melissa said.

By breakfast the next morning it seemed to Alex that almost everyone on campus had a copy of *Sports World*. Kids were reading the article in the line for breakfast and over orange juice and toast.

Kids were passing copies of *Sports World* around as they walked the campus. Kids were reading it out loud and discussing it with their friends.

When she got to the first class of the day where she knew she'd run into Dee, Alex took a couple of deep breaths before opening the classroom door. Come on, she told herself. She had to talk to Dee, had to congratulate her. She couldn't keep munching on sour grapes.

Dee was at her desk with a cluster of fans already around her. Even Mike was there. "Just incredible," said one girl to Dee. "I can't believe it."

"Have your parents called you yet?"

"No," Dee said. "I called them. I guess we got the first copies here. It hasn't arrived in Des Moines yet. So I told them about it, and my mother is set to hit all the drugstores in town and buy a million copies."

Alex stood outside the little group for a minute. "Hi, Alex," Mike said. "Pretty big story, wasn't it?"

"Yeah," Alex said. "It was wonderful. I can't believe it."

Dee saw her and was looking her way. If she were going to say something, it would have to be now.

"Dee," Alex said. "I can't believe it—the cover. You look fantastic."

"Thanks, Alex."

"The story was pretty great too."

Dee tossed her hair back. "It came as something of a shock," Dee said. "I was surprised they gave me so much space. There are so many other good people on the team. I wish they all could have gotten a story."

I'll bet you do, Alex thought. But she tried to give Dee a sincere-looking smile.

"Obviously they were very impressed with you," Alex said. "The coach had some nice things to say about you too."

"Right," Dee said, and turned away to talk to someone else.

"You want to go sit down?" Alex said, turning toward Mike.

"Yeah, just a minute," Mike said. "I got a couple questions I've got to ask Dee."

"Okay," Alex said. It looked as though even Mike were bowled over by Dee's stardom.

Alex spotted Melissa at the other side of the classroom and went and plunked her books down on a desk next to hers.

"You talk to Dee yet?" she asked Melissa.

"Yeah, I congratulated her."

"I wonder how long before this blows over?"

"I don't know," Alex said.

"Well, it won't be too soon for me," Melissa said.

Just then Danut walked into the classroom, spotted Alex, and sat down next to her. "Good morning, Alex," he said.

"Hello."

"Good morning, Melissa."

"Hello."

Since the pizza party at the Martins' house, Danut had started to mix in gradually with other students. He'd also taken to wearing jeans and sweaters like the rest of the kids.

"How do you like them?" he asked Alex.

"Like what?"

"These jeans. I picked them out myself this time. I thought you would notice right away."

"Oh, they're great."

"What is the problem?"

"It's the magazine cover."

"What magazine?"

"Sports World."

"Sports World?"

"You mean you haven't heard about it?" Melissa said. "You've got to be the only one on campus who doesn't know."

"You're forgetting, Melissa," Alex said. "Danut lives off campus with his mother. He doesn't hang around the dorms."

"What is this about *Sports World?*" Danut asked.

"It's the cover story," Alex said. "Dee is on the cover, and there's a big story inside about her and some other girls from the school."

"Now I shall guess," Danut said. "You and Dee are not getting along so well, and you are now feeling very jealous. Right?"

"Right so far," Alex said. "But I'm trying not to be."

"You Americans," Danut said. "You are so much wrapped up in being movie stars all the time."

"I don't want to be a movie star," Alex said. "I just want to be the best gymnast in the world—*and* I want everybody to know it."

She couldn't help but laugh at herself after she said that. Danut laughed with her.

"You will make it, Alex," he said, reaching across the aisle to pat her on the shoulder. "You will make it."

"I hope so," Alex said, letting out a big sigh.

Chapter Sixteen

The next day was Saturday, and Melissa and Alex decided to spend their free afternoon after practice taking in a matinee at a movie theater downtown.

"It really does feel wonderful to get away from campus, doesn't it?" Alex said.

"You still thinking about leaving Olympic High?"

"I don't know," Alex said. "I guess maybe I'm getting over it a little bit. It's probably too big a deal to change in the middle of the year. Maybe I'll wait until spring."

"Why don't we stop off for a Coke before we go back?" Melissa suggested as they passed a coffee shop. "We've got loads of time before dinner."

"Okay," Alex said, and together they pushed through the doors of the restaurant.

"Oh, my gosh," Melissa yelped as they stood at the doorway, looking for a place to sit down. "Over there in the corner booth—it's Mike and Dee."

At first Alex stared in disbelief. Then she realized it was true. It was Mike and Dee, their heads bent together over a banana split they were obviously sharing.

"Let's get out of here," she said to Melissa. "I don't want them to see me."

But it was too late. Mike, who was facing the door, had already looked up and seen her. He said something to Dee, then stood up with all the color draining out of his face.

Dee turned their way and smiled. "That crocodile," Melissa said. "She looks ready to devour us along with her ice cream."

Alex turned and started going out the door with Melissa following. They had taken only three steps, though, when she felt Mike pull on her elbow.

"Hey, wait a minute," Mike said. "I've got to explain something."

"What is there to explain?" Alex asked. "The two of you are obviously on a date. A chummy little afternoon coated with hot fudge and whipped cream with a maraschino cherry stuck on top."

"It's not exactly like that," Mike said.

"So what is it like?" Alex said, facing him squarely and planting her hands on her hips. Melissa stood a few steps away, obviously too shocked to move or say anything.

"We're just discussing the article that was in *Sports World*."

"I thought you did that yesterday in class."

"Well, now Dee's gotten a phone call from New York from the Olympic Committee. They want to make up posters of all the girls who were in the article and sell them to raise money for the Olympic team."

"Can you beat that!" Alex said. "Is she going to get you on a poster too?"

"Not exactly, but she was talking to somebody on the Olympic Committee about me, and they're also looking for some guys to do product endorsements. No money for me at all, you understand, but for the team. But you know how they work those things. Some of the money gets spent on the athlete's training. . . ."

"Funny that your name came immediately to mind when the Olympic Committee called her."

"What's that supposed to mean?"

"I guess I mean that I wonder how long the two of you have been seeing each other like this. Like, every Saturday afternoon?"

"Not really. Just once in a while. We're friends—all of us—you, me, Dee. At least we *were* friends until the two of you had that big argument and you moved out of your room."

"That's weird, Mike, because I always thought we were a lot more than friends, you and me."

Mike didn't say anything. He just scuffed at the ground with the toe of his tennis shoe.

She looked at him standing there with one arm resting against the window of the store that they were standing next to, and she remembered the times when he had taken her in his arms and kissed her. She wished that would happen again. She wished he would put his arm around her and tell her it was a big mistake.

But obviously that wasn't going to happen.

"Well, good luck with your sports career," Alex said, starting to walk away. "I just hope you don't stumble over the bodies as you claw your way to the top."

Mike didn't say anything as they turned away. Melissa looked back at him once or twice as Alex held on to her arm and pulled her down the sidewalk as quickly as she could.

"He's still standing there," Melissa said after the first glance. "No, now he's going back inside."

"So what?" Alex said. "We're finished."

They waited in silence for about five minutes for the bus to come. Once it arrived, Alex lurched on and plopped down on a seat.

"Well, that's really the last straw, isn't it?" Alex said. "On top of everything else she's stolen my boyfriend."

"What are you going to do about it?" Melissa asked.

"I'm going to beat her!" Alex said, biting off each word with a snap. "That invitational that's coming up—I'm going to make her look so bad that she'll never recover. And then I'm going to get out of this lousy school and never come back."

Chapter Seventeen

"I can't study around here anymore," Alex said the next afternoon as she tossed her book on her bed.

Out in the corridor there was music blaring, and somebody was running up and down the hallway.

"I'm going to the library," she told Melissa.

She threw her books into her book bag and headed out the door. Was it the noise, Alex wondered, or was it her own uneasiness and disappointment that was keeping her from concentrating?

It was a warm, sunny afternoon, unusual for Colorado in the winter, and the library was deserted. Olympic High students who worked around the clock all week in classrooms and the gym weren't likely to spend their only free day of the week studying.

But there, sitting on a couch in the reading room, was Danut Lescu.

Alex went and sat on a couch opposite him, opened her book, and tried to get involved in *The House of the Seven Gables*.

Her eyes moved over the lines of type, but her mind was really back on that downtown street outside the restaurant with Mike. Suddenly it all seemed so futile, so frustrating, and for the first time since everything had happened, she felt tears welling up in her eyes. One tear rolled down her cheek and made a big splotch in the middle of the page she was looking at.

She looked up and saw Danut staring at her. She grabbed her purse and ran out of the reading room. Danut followed and stopped her in the hall.

"Alex, what is wrong?"

"I never cry," she told him. "You're got to believe that I absolutely never cry. I'm not that kind of person. I'm really tough."

"I do believe it," Danut said. "That is what my mother is saying about you."

"Your mother talks about me?"

"She talks about all the girls all the time. So what is the matter?"

"I find this really hard to put into words, but you'll probably hear about it from somebody else. The whole school will know pretty soon, thanks to Dee."

"Know what?"

"It's about Mike and me and Dee. Apparently there's been a little love triangle going on without my knowing about it. Mike's been going out with me, but he's been seeing Dee, too, and yesterday I spotted the two of them downtown. Now that Dee got that big spread in *Sports World,* the balance seems to have tipped in her favor, and I think Mike is giving me up to concentrate on her."

"I wish I could say that I am sorry," Danut said, "but I am not."

"That's not very nice," Alex said, laughing through her tears.

"But you must understand, Alex," Danut said. "I'm not trying to be mean. I'm just glad to see the last of Mike, I guess. I don't know how Americans talk about these things, but I am—how do you say it?—crazy about you."

"Danut," Alex said, "I didn't realize ... You seemed to be making so many new friends. You hardly spoke to me for weeks."

"I suppose I had almost given up. So now, Alex, you must tell me how you feel about me."

Alex felt a warm rush of feelings that seemed to crowd out all the pain over Mike.

"I don't know," she said. "I guess I've tried to avoid you because of Mike, but I was really upset that night at the party when you spent the evening with all those other kids. I felt rejected."

"That's a good sign."

"Maybe. But, Danut, you don't understand one big problem. Your mother hates me, and she would never stand for it if we started seeing one another."

"Hates you?"

"Ever since she got to Olympic High she's been upset with me. It started that day outside Mr. Amundsen's office when I jumped out of the window. She thinks I'm an idiot, and ... and ... terrible at gymnastics. I'm ready to quit the school."

"But that is not smart. She does not hate you. She talks about you all the time. She says very nice things about you."

"She does? You're making that up."

"Really, Alex, you must believe me. She has told me over and over how tough you are, such a good worker. She has said that you needed more polish and refinement, but she also told me that you are capable of doing incredible things in gymnastics."

"But she said I was sloppy."

"That is right, sloppy about the details, but she is sure you could straighten all those things out."

"Well, why didn't she tell me all that herself?"

"She probably has tried to, but it is difficult to communicate to Americans when you are first starting out in this country."

Alex went back in her mind over some of the things that Mrs. Lescu had said to her in conferences and practices. It did seem to fit Danut's version of things a little bit.

"And one thing you should know about my mother, Alex, is that she is not very happy to be in this country. Back in Romania life for her was like for a movie producer or some president of a big company in this country. She was very famous—a celebrity—working very hard at something she loved to do and well paid for all that she did."

"So why did she come here, then?"

"It was just for me," Danut said. "She was worried that I did not get the right education. She also worried that I would not get a job after school in which I could really do the kind of research I want to do. She wanted me to have more freedom of choice.

"And on top of it all she was very upset about working with Americans. I guess in that way she was prejudiced against you and maybe against all of Olympic High. She has always considered Americans slipshod and sloppy in gymnastics. She was not looking forward to training American girls."

"And I fit that picture exactly, didn't I, jumping down off the roof?"

"Maybe a little bit," Danut said. "But I think she has sort of forgiven you for that. And now, maybe it's time for you to give her another chance too. Don't talk about leaving here, and don't think for a minute about that stupid magazine, *Sports World*. It's totally meaningless, that article. If you really love gymnastics, you should be doing it for your own sake, not for the press clippings, right?"

"Right," Alex said. "You are right."

"And can you forgive my mother her prejudices and give her another chance?"

"I'll have to see about that. I'm not totally sure."

"Well, I can serve as a sort of peace negotiator," Danut said, "between Eastern Europe and America. I shall talk to her too."

"You can't do that," Alex said. "I don't want you to do that."

"But why not?"

"I don't know," Alex said. "I guess I'd just be embarrassed to face her if you did."

"That is foolish, Alex. All the time I talk to her about you."

"You do?"

Danut reached out and put his arm around Alex's shoulders. "I know it's going to take some time for you to get used to me—how do you say?—hanging around all the time, but you are willing to give me a chance, too, aren't you?"

"Okay," Alex said, wiping her eyes with a tissue and smiling up at Danut. "I'd like that."

Chapter Eighteen

"Wasn't that Danut Lescu that I saw walking with you out of the library yesterday?" Angela Avery asked Alex as they walked into gymnastics practice the next afternoon.

"That's right," Alex said. "Actually we weren't just together at the library, either. We went downtown for a hamburger afterward, and you can tell that to Dee, too, if you feel like it."

"Don't be so touchy," Angela said. "I was just asking. I guess you're really through with Mike now, huh?"

"So how many other people have gotten the word from you and Dee by now?"

"Alex, it's been all over the school for a long time now. You were absolutely the last person to find out about it. I mean, Mike has been chasing after Dee for absolutely weeks."

Alex felt her face getting red. She wanted more than anything to reach out and pull Angela's dishwater-blond ponytail until she yelled uncle.

"No kidding," she said as coolly as she could.

"There were even a couple of times when he went out with you, brought you back to the dorm, and then picked up Dee for a date. Of course, Dee was just totally in a quandary. She didn't know what to do. I mean, she was your best friend at the time, and she didn't want to hurt you. But here he was—positively wild about her—and she seemed to be falling for him too."

"Angela," Alex said, "why are you telling me all this? Do you want to make me feel really bad or something, even worse than I felt already? Or maybe Dee told you to do it? Maybe she wanted to pay me back for something or other?"

"Really, Alex," Angela said, "You're so sensitive. I just thought you'd want to know, that's all. I thought maybe it would make you feel a little better to know that it was—like—inevitable, that it didn't just happen in one Saturday afternoon."

"Thanks, Angela," Alex said. "I get the picture. And you might tell Dee for me that it's not over between her and me yet. She may have walked away with Mr. Muscles, but I'm going to even up the score. In fact, before this is finished, I'm going to walk all over her."

"What's that supposed to mean?" Angela said. "You must know that Dee and Mike are really a firm item these days. No way you're going to pry him away from her."

"Get away from me, Angela. I don't want to talk about it anymore."

Angela tossed her head and trotted off to a group around the uneven bars, which included Dee. As Alex had expected, she went straight to Dee, and she could see them whispering together.

Alex shook her head and went to work on the balance beam.

She was going to get over Mike, she decided. In fact, she really didn't miss having him hanging around all the time. In class, of course, it was a little embarrassing seeing him. Once he had almost run into her in the hall. He had said a polite hello; she said nothing—just nodded her head.

And then there was Danut. He hadn't been all over her or tried to crowd in to take up where Mike left off. But he had sat next to her in one of her classes and told her some funny stories about Mr. Amundsen and his mother. She'd even found herself laughing out loud. Imagine that, there she was on the brink of a major personal tragedy and she was still able to laugh.

But she knew she'd never be able to forgive Dee. She'd never forget the deception—trying to push Alex into a backseat on the team. Now it was hard for her to believe that they had ever been friends.

Alex had been working on the medium-height beam for about twenty minutes when she noticed Mrs. Lescu standing nearby, watching her.

Alex went through the routine perfectly, she thought, and then dismounted and came down onto the mats so that Melissa could try her routine.

"Excellent progress, Alex," Mrs. Lescu said. "You should probably have that ready in time for the invitational next week."

"You think I can do it?"

"You have shown great improvement," was all that Mrs. Lescu said back.

"She's not exactly what I'd call a warm and affectionate personality, is she?" Melissa said as Mrs. Lescu walked away.

"No, I guess she's got a real problem communicating with people," Alex said.

As the coach had promised, she had Alex practicing her routine on the performance-height bar, forty-eight inches above the floor, by the next day. Alex found that there were almost no problem parts left as she went through the movements in the routine. Everything was very smooth, very tight, under control.

"I'm not doing too badly at anything else, either, am I?" Alex asked Melissa.

"You've been fantastic on the bars and the vault this week," Melissa said. "You're going to really smash them at this meet."

"That's exactly what I'm planning to do," Alex said.

During the last few days of practice before the meet, which was going to be held in California, Alex tried to keep an eye on Dee's progress. The coach still seemed to be paying a lot of attention to Dee, Alex thought. But she was sure that she was outdoing Dee now on every piece of equipment. Dee was still having some problems with the balance beam routine that was so similar to Alex's. In fact, the coach hadn't let her perform it on the high beam yet.

"This really looks like it's going to be my meet," Alex said during one practice while watching Dee stumble on a turn on the beam.

Finally, two days before the meet, Mrs. Lescu came and watched Alex do her balance beam routine three times through.

"Well, Alex, I believe you have wrapped it up," she said. "Do you want to do this in California?"

"Absolutely," Alex said, almost bouncing along the mats as she walked up to Mrs. Lescu. "I'm dying to do it."

"It's spectacular," Mrs. Lescu said, "but every minute you must keep in mind—legs straight, toes pointed, body graceful like a swan. No sloppy slipups, or all these wonderful things you can do will mean nothing."

"I can do it," Alex said, "and I will do it."

As Mrs. Lescu walked away Alex told Melissa, "That's the closest thing to an out-and-out compliment she's ever given me."

Chapter Nineteen

The team was going to fly to California for the meet on a Friday morning. On Thursday Alex met Danut in class. "Would it bother you very much if I flew out there and showed up for the optionals part of the meet?" he asked her.

"It wouldn't bother me at all. It would be wonderful," Alex said. "Actually I wish you could come out with the whole team when it leaves tomorrow. It's going to be horrible flying with Dee and Mike and Angela—all of us locked up inside the same airplane."

"Alex," Danut said, "you must start putting all of that out of your mind."

"You're right," Alex said. "But it still bothers me sometimes. After this meet I know I'll feel a lot better, especially after smashing Dee."

"Alex!"

Alex laughed, but she knew that inside her head that was exactly how she felt. She had to smash Dee at this meet and every meet thereafter.

"So how come you're going to the meet?" Alex said.

"Well, it is to see you, of course. But it is also because of my mother. This is her first meet in this country on the American side. I want to be there to encourage her so she isn't feeling so alone. And how do the two of you get along these days?"

"A little better," Alex said. "We're still not best friends, of course, but it's improving. I guess you've had something to do with that."

"Perhaps just a little bit," Danut said.

On Friday Alex and Melissa and the rest of the team had to get up at five for an early breakfast. Then they all crowded onto a school bus for a ride to the Denver airport where they were to catch the plane.

Alex and Melissa took a seat in the rear of the bus, and Alex sat by the window where she thought she could try to ignore Dee and Mike, who got on the bus as a couple and sat together with Angela in a seat right in back of them.

The bus bumped and jounced all the way, but Alex managed to doze off for about half an hour of the one-hour trip to the airport. Her stomach felt queasy and nervous, partly because of the meet coming up, partly because of the presence of Dee and Mike on the bus.

They arrived at the airport with just a little time to spare, and Mrs. Lescu quickly hustled them to get seats assigned at a counter and then onto the plane.

Alex groaned as she and Melissa walked up to their assigned seats. This time they were right across the aisle from Dee and Mike.

"Maybe we should get these seats switched," Alex said to Melissa. "I don't know if I can stand this."

"Oh, it's okay," Melissa said. "You sit by the window, I'll sit by them on the aisle."

They stuffed their gear in the overhead compartment, and Alex went and got some magazines from the front of the plane.

"It's only an hour or two in the air," Melissa said. "Just breathe deeply and try to ignore them."

"I don't know if I can," Alex said. "Look at them."

Dee was cuddled up in her seat with her shoulder leaning against Mike. "Oh, Mike," she said in a sugary-sweet tone of voice, "I'm so nervous about this meet."

"You'll do fine," Mike said, patting Dee's hand.

"She ought to be nervous," Alex muttered to Melissa.

A couple of times Dee sent Mike up to the front of the plane—to get her a magazine, an aspirin, a glass of water.

"Good grief," Melissa said to Mike as he returned from one of his errands for Dee, "the airline ought to pay you a salary for all the work you're doing."

Mike laughed; Dee glared at Melissa and Alex.

Alex got up and walked to the back of the airplane to use the rest room. When she came back out, the little door opened and practically hit Dee in the face.

"Excuse me," Alex said. "You shouldn't have been standing so close."

"Standing close?" Dee said. "I wasn't standing close. You shouldn't have come busting out of there like that, that's all."

"Look, Dee," Alex said. "I think the two of us should keep our distance, if you know what I mean. I want to be as polite as possible. I don't want to cause a fuss."

"That's really cute," Dee said. "You and Melissa sit over there making nasty remarks, and you say you want to be polite. You're one of the rudest people I've ever met."

"We aren't talking about you," Alex said. "Melissa said one thing, made one little joke, and you get all upset about it."

"You just can't stand it, can you?" Dee said. "You're just green with envy. First I get on the cover of *Sports World,* then Mike falls for me. You can't believe that the whole world doesn't revolve around Alexandra Hays anymore. You can't believe that any other gymnast in the world could get the kind of recognition that you got."

Alex grabbed the back of a seat in front of her while the airplane started to bobble and bounce. Red lights were flashing all over the plane, warning passengers to buckle their seat belts. The plane must have been about to land. She felt as if red lights were flashing inside her head as well.

"Dee," Alex said, "you just don't understand. The whole world does revolve around me. It always has and it always will. When we get to this meet, you're going to find that out. I'm going to beat you so bad you'll never forget it. And then the whole school will know—everyone in gymnastics is going to know—who's really on top. You got that straight?"

A stewardess had walked up to them by now and had taken Dee by the arm. "We've got to all sit down, miss," she said. "The plane's about to land."

She tugged at Dee's elbow, and Dee walked back with her. She looked back over her shoulder, though, at Alex. "Why don't you just give up, Alex? You're going to be totally surprised. If you think you're going to get Mike back that way, you're completely mistaken."

"I don't want Mike back," Alex said.

As soon as Dee was in her seat Alex went back to hers.

She refused to look in Dee and Mike's direction.

"What was all that about?" Melissa asked. "You could hear it all over the plane."

"It was a pretty bad scene, wasn't it?" Alex said. "I wish I hadn't gotten started like that, but it's too late now. She just keeps rubbing me the wrong way."

"I think she's crying now," Melissa whispered to her a couple of minutes later.

Alex, who had her eyes closed and her head back, could hear Dee blowing her nose.

"Mike is comforting her," Melissa said.

"I'll bet he is."

Chapter Twenty

The meet was held at a giant gym in Los Angeles with what seemed to be hundreds of girls competing.

When the Olympic High team arrived at the gymnasium early in the day, only a few people were there other than the performers, coaches, officials, and judges. The air in the huge building felt cold and damp to Alex, even through her warm-up suit.

With the other girls she went to an adjacent room next to the performance area where there was equipment similar to that they would use in competition. The teams took turns warming up.

The first day of the meet would be devoted to compulsory exercises. And the second would have the voluntaries or optionals—the performances that included the most spectacular movements like the balance beam routine that Alex had been working on for so long.

Dee had an advantage in the compulsories, Alex thought as she took some practice swings on the uneven bars. The required movements that made up compulsories were less difficult, and more emphasis was put on execution, style, and grace—never Alex's strong points. At least not until now, she thought. This time things would be different.

With so many competitors it was going to be hard to keep track of what Dee was doing. But that was all right with Alex. She didn't want to slavishly follow every point. That would just make her nervous. All she knew was that at the end of the day she had to come out only slightly behind Dee or else she couldn't hope to catch up and pass her in the optionals.

Before the events began, the girls on the team all sat at the sidelines where Mrs. Lescu talked to them. Everyone was totally silent and looked a little grim. "You have all made tremendous advances in past few weeks," Mrs. Lescu said. "I expect the very best from all of you. This meet not terribly important, but it is good chance for you to begin the road to the Olympics. It would not surprise me if every spot on the Olympic team next year would be filled with girls from Olympic High."

Alex found out that she would open on the uneven bars. She taped her hands and wrists and heavily chalked her hands, which were already beginning to feel sweaty and slippery. Then, as performer after performer went onto the bars ahead of her, she stretched at the sidelines or paced back and forth. She felt the adrenaline pumping inside of her. It made her feel light and giddy in her head and tense in her diaphragm. She closed her eyes and tried to picture what she would do on the bars. She wanted to go out there now and get it over with. She didn't want to wait.

Then it was her turn. Mrs. Lescu walked up to her and patted her on the back. In a few seconds she was up in the air, swinging, spinning, twisting, catching the bars as if she had magnets on her hands. Then she was releasing and catching again. A whirling dismount and she was on the mat in a perfect landing.

A few seconds later, the judges flashed her score on the electronic board: 9.95 out of a perfect 10. Exactly where she wanted to be, maybe a little better.

The rest of the day passed quickly. Event after event rolled by, and Alex felt as if she were a machine, a robot performing with perfect precision.

When it was over, she felt on the verge of collapse. Her knees were weak; her hair was a mess; her body felt covered with chalk and sweat.

She sank onto a chair with the rest of the team after the scoreboard again flashed a 9.95 for her floor exercises.

"You're ahead of her, you know," Melissa said as Alex sat down next to her.

"Ahead? That's impossible. I've never beaten her in the compulsories before."

"It's just a hair, 39.9 for you and 39.45 for her," Melissa said, "but with that behind you, you can smash her tomorrow. And by the way, I think you're ahead of everybody else in the entire meet too."

Even Mrs. Lescu came over a few minutes later to pat Alex on the back. After she had gone, Alex leaned forward and sneaked a glance at Dee. Dee also looked totally disheveled and worn-out. It had been a hard day for everyone. A twinge of guilt passed through her as she looked at Dee's tired eyes. Even the fabulous, never-mussed Deirdre Winters hairdo looked a little limp. Alex leaned back and let herself relax. She was on top this time. She could feel it.

That night the whole team went to dinner in the hotel dining room, and Alex was ravenous. She did hold back, though, from eating her baked potato, and she passed on dessert. She wasn't going to let an extra ounce of fat spoil the next day for her.

When they'd finished eating, she and Melissa went upstairs to their room where they planned an evening of TV watching and an early bedtime. Throughout dinner, though, and as they sat through a string of situation comedies for a couple of hours, Alex couldn't stop going over and over in her mind her routine on the balance beam. She hoped she wouldn't draw that event first. She needed time tomorrow to loosen up, to get ready.

Tomorrow Danut would be there too, she remembered. That gave her a warm feeling in spite of her jitters. He would be there cheering for her if nobody else was.

Melissa stood up. "I'm restless," she said. "I'm going down the hall to find out what's happening."

"You ought to get to bed soon," Alex said. "You didn't do too shabby a job yourself today, and you need to rest up for tomorrow."

Melissa smiled. "I did do okay, didn't I?"

"You mind if I turn out the lights and go to bed before you get back?" Alex asked. "I'll leave the light on in the bathroom for you so you'll be able to see."

Melissa nodded and was out the door.

After Melissa left Alex couldn't sleep. She had started to worry that she might end up staying awake all night when the door clicked open and Melissa walked in.

"Alex," she said softly, "you still awake?"

"Yes," Alex said, sitting up and turning on the bedroom light. "I can't sleep, I'm too nervous."

"You're not going to believe this," Melissa said. "But I just found out that Dee plans to use her new routine on the balance beam in tomorrow's optionals."

"That's impossible," Alex said. "She hasn't been able to stick it yet in practice."

"Maybe not, but I guess she figures that if she changes it a little bit, takes out one or two of the problem parts, she'll be able to come up with something that will really dazzle the judges."

"That is so crazy!" Alex said. "The coach would never let her do that. Mrs. Lescu demands perfection before she lets somebody try something new—especially for a meet."

"She's not going to tell the coach. After all, once she's up there on the beam, Mrs. Lescu can't run out there and pull her off, can she?"

"Who told you all this?" Alex asked.

"Angela," Melissa said. "You know Angela. She can never keep her mouth shut about anything. She's told a whole bunch of people already. I'm not the first."

"Well, maybe it will get back to the coach."

"I doubt it," Melissa said. "The kids don't exactly confide in Mrs. Lescu."

"But why's she doing all this? At the very least she could fall off and ruin her score—plus she might really hurt herself."

"It's obvious, isn't it?" Melissa said. "She's determined to beat you in this meet, and she figures she has to take a gamble if she's going to."

"That's nuts," Alex said. "I might want to beat her pretty badly myself, but I'd never take a chance like that."

"You wouldn't?" Melissa said. "I'm not so sure about that. Look at how badly you've been feeling about Dee lately. If you were the one who was behind and it looked like you might lose, you just might try the same kind of thing."

Alex didn't know what to say to that. Maybe Melissa was right; maybe she would try the same thing. Coming into this meet, Alex had been pretty bitter about Dee and what she thought Dee had done to her. Now that the meet was under way and she had gotten some of her confidence back, she didn't feel so upset anymore. In fact, almost all the bitterness was drained out of her.

She went over and over it in her mind for the next couple of hours, long after they'd turned out the lights and Melissa was breathing evenly and deeply in the bed next to hers.

How had she and Dee ended up this way? she wondered. There had to be more to it than *Sports World* and Mike; the seeds of bad feelings between them went back a long way. There had always been that edge of competitiveness to their friendship—the feeling that they were neck and neck and had to beat each other out. But now it had gotten totally out of hand. And it seemed that Dee was ready to try anything to win.

Chapter Twenty-One

Alex woke up about an hour before she needed to the next morning. She took a shower and got dressed while Melissa still slept.

"What are you doing?" Melissa said, leaning up in bed on one arm to look at Alex brushing out her hair and then tying it back in a ponytail.

"I've got to go talk to Dee," Alex said. "I've got to see her before the meet."

"That won't do any good," Melissa said.

"Maybe not," Alex said, "but I've at least got to give it a try."

She finished off her hair, grabbed a jacket, pulled it over her leotard top, and went to the door.

"I'll meet you downstairs for breakfast in half an hour," she said as she went.

She went down the hall to the room where Dee and Angela were staying. She paused at the door. Could she go through with this? She knocked.

No answer.

Everybody was still in bed probably. She knocked again, harder this time.

A chain jangled against the door, the lock clicked, and the door opened a crack. It was Dee, in her nightgown with her hair hanging loosely down around her shoulders.

"Alex," Dee said. "What are you doing here?"
"Can I talk to you for a minute?" Alex asked.
"Why?"
"Could I come in for just a second?"

Dee sighed and opened the door. She went and got a bathrobe and came back. "What is it now?" Dee asked. "We could have slept for another half hour if you hadn't started pounding down the door. You really have a lot of nerve."

"I won't stay long," Alex said. "I'm just sort of nervous about the meet today."

"Why? You're ahead," Dee said. "That's nothing to be nervous about."

"I heard something last night that got me sort of upset."

"And what was that?"

"It's Angela," Alex said, nodding in the direction of Angela, who was still snoozing under the covers. "She's been telling everyone that you're thinking of trying your new routine on the balance beam at this meet."

"And so what if I am?" Dee said. "Like I told you before, that routine of yours isn't private property. Besides that, I've changed it. It won't be exactly the same as yours. No one's even going to notice."

"No, I'm sure they won't. But that's not what's bothering me. I mean, you're right, probably nobody will remember who did what. It's all in how you do it, anyway, right?"

"Right! So if we've got that settled, then you can be on your way so we can get back to sleep."

Dee started walking toward the door.

"But, Dee," Alex said, "the problem is—you're not ready to do that routine yet, are you? What if it doesn't work out?"

146

"Alex, if this is supposed to be some kind of joke or something, I really don't appreciate it. I can handle my own career, thanks. I don't need any coaching from you."

"Are you going to talk to Mrs. Lescu about it?"

"That's up to me to decide, Alex. It's none of your business. And you'd better not say anything to her."

"I won't, but I just wish you'd change your mind. We used to be friends, Dee. I'm sorry things have gotten so far out of hand. I just don't want this meet to turn into a disaster for you."

"Alex, you and I both know that you're afraid of me and what I can do to you out there today. The only reason you're trying to talk me out of doing that routine is that you think I'm going to beat you."

"Maybe you will beat me," Alex said. "But you'll be taking a big chance."

"I'm sick of you, Alex. I'm sick of coming in second to you all the time. Lately things have been changing for me, and they're going to keep on changing. And as far as I'm concerned, this meet is just another one of those turnarounds."

"I guess I'd better leave," Alex said.

"I think so."

Dee turned her back to Alex, and Alex went to the door.

"I'm sorry, Dee. I wish you wouldn't try it."

When Alex was out in the hall, she heard Dee come to the door and yell after her, "You'd better not say anything to the coach, Alex, or you'll really be sorry."

Chapter Twenty-Two

"So *are* you going to say something to the coach?" Melissa asked Alex as they sat at the side of the gym after their warm-ups and waited for the optional performances to start.

"How could I?" Alex said. "Then she'd *never* forgive me. It's just an impossible situation."

"Maybe you could talk to Danut," Melissa said. "Here he comes now."

Danut Lescu was dodging among groups of people and walking across the gym toward the Olympic High team. His mother stood up when she saw him coming and kissed him on the cheek. He talked to her for a few minutes and then walked up to Alex.

He sat down in the chair next to her. "All set?" he asked. "My mother tells me the good news. You had a tremendous day yesterday, yes?"

Alex smiled. "It was wonderful. I'm leading everyone in my class. Not by much, of course. Dee is right behind me."

"I'm sure that it is for you just the beginning, Alex. You are sitting on top of the world now."

"I've got a long way to go, though, and first I've got to work really hard today."

Should she tell Danut about Dee? Alex wondered. Somehow she felt she couldn't. If he went to his mother and Dee found out about it, it could turn into a big mess. No, she would just have to sit tight and see what Dee did.

Maybe she would go talk to Dee about it one more time. Danut left to go sit in the audience seats, which were rapidly filling up, and Alex slipped down to where Dee was sitting.

"Dee, have you thought about what we talked about this morning?"

Dee looked up at her. "I really don't know what you mean, Alex, and I don't want to talk about it."

"Have you talked to Mike about it?" Alex nodded toward the men's gymnastics events going on at the other end of the gym.

"Alex," Dee snapped, "just stay out of this!"

"Okay," Alex said. "I just wanted to check."

As it turned out, both she and Dee were to perform with the same group of girls, first in the floor exercises, then in the vault and on the uneven bars, and finally on the balance beam.

Great, Alex thought to herself, now I get to feel guilty about Dee all day long.

Just before the performances were about to begin she sat down on a chair, closed her eyes, and tried to concentrate on the apparatus, on what she was going to do, on shutting out the noise of the crowd around her.

It was as if she were turning on a movie camera in her head and then watching herself run through the floor exercises. In her mind she pictured herself doing perfect handsprings and somersaults that almost touched the ceiling as she hummed her performance music.

After a few moments she opened her eyes, and the noises and sight of the people around her assaulted her senses again. All the peace and quiet was gone. Pretty soon it was her turn to perform.

She rolled her shoulders, shook her thighs, stretched a few times, and went out to the floor.

Once out there she felt totally alone—as if she were the only person in the gymnasium. All thoughts of Dee, of Danut, of Mrs. Lescu were far away. Her mind was fixed totally on the twelve square meters of space she had to perform in, on staying inside those boundaries, on finishing exactly in the minute and a half or so allotted to her, on not getting ahead of the music, on not starting too soon, on keeping her legs straight, her toes pointed, her angles just right.

She signaled to the judges that she was ready to start and that they should turn on her music.

After the first few notes began, she was off, beginning with a high double-back somersault in the lay-out, or stretched-out-flat position. She felt herself soaring, twisting higher than she ever had before.

A dance segment came next, and she extended her arms and legs in what she hoped were more elegant, swanlike lines than she had ever achieved before. Be like Dee, she told herself, be graceful.

In between the leaps and splits that followed there were three other versions of double-backs. Then there was a final set of dancelike movements and the music stopped.

She could hear the clapping from members of the team, and she went down off the platform to hugs from Melissa and Beth.

"Look at that score," Melissa said. A 9.9—her average of the judges' scores with the highest and lowest dropped—flashed on the scoreboard.

Alex knew she should be excited, but she felt strangely numb, as if it were someone performing other than herself.

"She's keeping right up with you, though," Melissa whispered. "She got the very same score, which is surprising considering that she usually starts falling behind in the voluntaries."

Alex knew Melissa was talking about Dee and how Dee had done in the floor exercises a little earlier. But suddenly how Dee did in these events didn't seem to matter anymore. Alex knew she was going to win. The anger was gone.

She glanced in Dee's direction and saw the other girl slumped in her chair with her face set in a gray mask.

The uneven bars and the vault seemed to pass by more quickly this time, and again Alex notched up almost perfect scores that were tied by Dee's scores.

"I can't belive this," Melissa said as they prepared for the last event—the balance beam. "I was sure she would be behind by now."

"With the score so close," Alex said, "I guess she's going to try it, isn't she? I mean, if I had been way ahead or she had been way ahead, she might have held off."

"Right," Melissa said, "she probably thinks that she's got to do something spectacular if she's going to match you or do better than you on the balance beam."

"I'm starting to feel really terrible," Alex said. "She just can't go through with this."

"Stop thinking about her," Melissa said. "You've got to think about yourself. Forget Dee. Wipe her out of your mind."

That's exactly what she would have to do, Alex

thought. She would have to stop worrying about Dee or she would go crazy.

She and Dee were scheduled to perform back to back. First Dee, then Alex. Performances by the other girls passed by Alex as if she were watching them on television. She couldn't concentrate. After all, it was between Dee and her now.

Dee was ready now, and she went up to the beam performance area. Her lips were pressed into a tight line. Her eyes were narrowed. Her chin jutted out in a combative way.

"She really looks determined, doesn't she?" Alex said to Melissa.

Dee got a signal from the judges that she could start, and her whole body seemed to tighten like a compressed spring. When Alex saw her go into a roundoff onto the board next to the beam, she knew that Dee was going ahead with the new routine. Alex glanced toward Mrs. Lescu. The coach stood up, her mouth open.

"I guess this is it," Melissa said. "Mrs. Lescu looks pretty surprised."

"I can't watch," Alex gasped as Dee went into an aerial that didn't seem quite high enough. She turned her head away and closed her eyes, and a second later she heard gasps and groans of shock from the crowd.

"Oh, no," Melissa said, "she fell."

Alex stood up to look. It was true—Dee was lying in a crumpled heap on the mats. "I should have told Mrs. Lescu. I should have stopped her," Alex said. "I knew she couldn't do it."

A crowd of officials had rushed up to the balance beam, including Mrs. Lescu.

Alex felt tears starting in her eyes. "This is all my fault," Alex said. "All this fighting, this constant competing. If it wasn't for me, it would never have happened."

Alex ran up to the group clustered around Dee. Suddenly the crowd parted to let in two men with white coats who were carrying a stretcher. Dee still looked as if she hadn't moved. Her eyes were closed and her limbs were limp. "Do you think she's paralyzed or something?" Melissa whispered to Alex.

The men carried Dee out, and Mrs. Lescu followed them. Before the coach went out the gym door, though, she stopped and ran back to the group by the side of the gym. "I am sorry, Alex," she said. "I will not be able to stay for your performance. I must go with Dee to the hospital. I know this is terrible thing to happen just before you perform, but you must be strong now. Shut it out of your mind and keep going. It won't happen to you, too, you know. You are well prepared. Dee did something very foolish; she was not ready for the maneuvers she was trying to perform."

"But I feel terrible," Alex said. "Dee was just trying to beat me, and that's why she forced herself to do that routine."

"Put it out of your mind," Mrs. Lescu said in a loud, severe tone. "You must go on. The judges are almost ready for you."

Alex walked back to the chair she had been sitting in. Danut was standing there. He had come down out of the audience.

He put his arm around her shoulders, and she sagged against him. "Oh, Danut, it's all my fault. She could be badly hurt, and it's all because of me."

"Don't be ridiculous," he said. "You did not make her go up on there and try that."

Melissa ran up to them. "Alex, you've got to get up there. It's time. They're waiting for you," she said, panting.

"I can't go," Alex said. "I can't do it. I've got to get out of here!"

Danut put his hands on her shoulders and shook her. "Alex, you must perform. You must finish. You can't stop now. Take a couple of deep breaths and get out there."

Alex closed her eyes and sucked in deep swallows of air. She knew Danut was right. She had to go on. She wasn't the type who gave up, especially not when she was this close to an almost total victory at this meet. She walked evenly and slowly up to the balance beam and tried to picture in her mind exactly what steps, what maneuvers she would go through in her routine. The picture of Dee lying there kept coming back in her mind, and she shook her head, as if she were tossing the image away from her. She was going to do this perfectly. Nothing was going to stop her.

Before taking her spot for the opening she quickly ran through in her mind the routine she was going to perform—the routine she had been practicing for so long, the one she and Dee had been fighting over.

She focused hard on her opening and on the roundoff and back handspring onto the beam. Her timing had to be totally precise. If she were too early or too late, she could miss the beam, destroying her performance and perhaps hurting herself as well—just like Dee. No, she said to herself, don't think about Dee.

She chalked her hands heavily. Her palms were already beginning to feel sweaty. She checked her slippers to be sure they were securely tight on her feet.

She took her position, saluted the judges, went through some quick ballet movements, and took off with a tremendous burst of power. She was into the roundoff and then a perfect set of aerials. It had begun. She felt as if she were passing across the beam in slow motion, as if time were crawling by. She was moving by instinct now, as if the movements she had to make had been implanted in her mind since she was born.

Although she had been performing all day she felt strangely alive and strong, no weakness in her muscles, no feeling of fatigue.

Everything flowed smoothly, and as she passed through her dance movements she felt her hands, her arms, extending and arching with elegance. She tried to smile and look relaxed, as if she were performing on the floor instead of above ground. Then she was into the final set of aerials—the twisting, the curling. With a final explosion of her muscles she landed perfectly on the mat. A few more movements and her hands were in the air in triumph.

As she walked to the sidelines the other kids were all over her, yelling and patting her on the back. She could hardly feel or hear it. Now she felt tired, exhausted, drained, ready to rest.

She had done it. And when the perfect 10 flashed on the scoreboard seconds later, it was almost an anticlimax, though she joyously joined in the screaming this time and hugged Melissa, who had tears in her eyes. "You were so wonderful," Melissa said.

Then Danut was there, and she fell into his arms. "I did it, didn't I?" she said.

Chapter Twenty-Three

The hospital lobby, with its pale green enameled walls and pocked linoleum floors, seemed cold and damp to Alex. She kept her coat on while she sat and waited to talk to Mrs. Lescu. Danut sat across from her and thumbed through one magazine after another.

Right after the meet had ended Alex had gotten her first-place medal. She had gone through the awards ceremony as if in a dream. All she could think about was Dee, lying there next to the balance beam.

Then, as quickly as they could, Alex and Danut had gotten in a taxi and rushed to the hospital. Alex was still in her leotard and warm-up suit, and she had put a coat on over it as they had left the meet.

Once they'd found the right floor in the hospital, a nurse had taken word to Mrs. Lescu that they were there.

"What do you think?" Alex said to Danut. "Do you think she's hurt bad?"

"It is going to be all right," Danut said. "She will need a little time."

After about a half hour of waiting Mrs. Lescu came down the hall. Alex had been pacing the floor and was the first to see her.

Alex rushed to Mrs. Lescu. "Is she all right?" she asked. "What's the matter? How bad is it?"

Mrs. Lescu's hair was mussed, her eyes looked tired, and the edges of her mouth sagged. Her coat was open and unbuttoned and hung loosely around her.

"Now she has consciousness," the coach said. "She woke up one half an hour ago. Somehow she bumped her head as she came off the beam. And, thanks to God, nothing else is hurt. No broken bones or torn cartilage. No torn muscles. Just a small concussion."

"She's not paralyzed, then," Alex said, sighing in relief. She sank back down into one of the orange plastic chairs in the lobby.

"No, thanks to God," Mrs. Lescu said, sitting down herself next to Alex. "It is nothing like that. Just a minor injury. She will be out of the hospital in some few days."

"Mrs. Lescu," Alex said, "I've got to tell you something. It's about Dee and me and why this happened."

Mrs. Lescu looked up at Alex with a puzzled expression.

Alex covered her face with her hands. "I don't know how to start, but I want to tell the whole truth. It really began when you came to the school. It wasn't your fault, but somehow Dee and I started getting angry at each other. I guess it was mainly me. I thought that you were giving her all the attention in workouts and that you favored her over me. So I got upset, and I had a couple of fights with Dee.

"We both started working on those balance beam routines, and they were sort of similar, and I thought she was trying to steal my movements from me. I know that sounds silly, but somehow I felt as if it were a special routine that I developed just for myself."

Mrs. Lescu shook her head.

"Anyway, then Mike Schultz and *Sports World* got into it, and it ended up with me telling her that she could never beat me at this meet. I had a big fight with her on the airplane, and I was determined to smash her. So I guess she thought that she had to pull off this routine in order to show me. I feel terrible about all of this, and I could understand if you blamed me for it."

Mrs. Lescu patted Alex's shoulder. "My dear girl, I am so sorry. But it is not entirely your fault. Dee has to bear a lot of the blame in this. She knows now that she should never have let her feelings get away from her. She knows she should never have tried this. She was not ready to perform that routine. That I had told her myself just a few days ago."

"It's not like her, you know, to do something crazy like this," Alex said. "She was always the levelheaded one, more timid than I. I was always the one who jumped in first and then thought about it afterward, like that day on the balcony."

"One thing I realize now," Mrs. Lescu said, "is that I have some blame too. You are right. I did favor Dee. She reminded me very much of someone I worked with in Romania, a girl I loved very much. I felt drawn to her naturally. Her work was so much the same. You know who I mean, do you not, Danut?"

Danut nodded.

"So you see," Mrs. Lescu went on, "I let my feelings get away from me too. I let them influence my work so that someone get hurt."

Alex caught hold of Mrs. Lescu's hand and squeezed it. It shocked her that she and the coach were able to talk this way together. Alex found herself beginning to realize what it was like for Mrs. Lescu to come to a foreign country, to start over again with a strange group of athletes.

"Could I go in and see her?" Alex asked. "Could I just talk to her for a moment?"

"I think so," Mrs. Lescu said. "Mike Schultz is with her now."

Alex went down the hall with a nurse and into Dee's room. Dee was lying in bed, and Mike was sitting in a chair next to her, holding her hand. Mike nodded at Alex. "Hi, Alex," he said.

"Hello, Mike," Alex said. "I won't be here long, I just wanted to talk to Dee for a minute."

"Sure," Mike said. "I think Dee wants to talk to you too."

Dee's pale face was framed by bandages across her forehead. She looked weak and small lying against the big white pillow.

"You doing okay?" Alex asked.

Dee slowly turned her head and gave Alex a weak smile. "I guess so. I guess you were right, Alex. I shouldn't have tried that routine, should I?"

"No, not yet, anyway. But you'll be doing it one of these days."

"Maybe."

"I don't want to bother you," Alex said, staring at the toes of her tennis shoes. "I feel horrible, though. I feel so responsible for what's happened."

"Don't, Alex. Please don't."

"I just want you to know that I'm sorry for everything that's gone on between us over the past couple of months."

"I'm sorry too."

"I didn't want it to end up this way with one of us getting hurt. I don't know if things will ever be the same between us again, but I'd like to try to be friends."

"So would I. I guess I let things get kind of out of hand. It's hard sometimes, though, when you're always looking up to someone and you think you're never going to beat them."

"I'm beginning to realize that," Alex said. She reached out and took Dee's hand.

"Of course," Dee said with a soft little laugh, "this doesn't mean that you're always going to be on top."

"No, you're right," Alex said. "Somebody's bound to come along and beat me someday."

"And it just might be me," Dee said.

"Hey, wait a minute," Alex said. "I thought you'd learned your lesson."

Dee laughed and Alex smiled.

Danut was waiting for Alex outside the hospital room when she came out. They walked down the hall together toward the lobby and his mother. "You know what, Danut?" Alex said. "I think this is going to turn out all right, after all."